**"I'm going to make love to you."
Peter whispered the words against
the corner of her mouth.**

Jane shook her head, envisioning her naked
body tangled with Peter's. It couldn't be as
good as she imagined it would be. And making
love to him would only commit her deeper into
the relationship. She didn't want to fall in love
with him.

Bitter experience had taught Jane that she
was better off alone. Unloved. But the words
sounded hollow, even though she spoke them
only to herself.

"No," she told him.

Peter didn't look convinced. "Soon," he
countered. "For now I'm going to kiss you...."

Kristine Rolofson continues to delight her many fans with her warm and moving love stories. A resident of Rhode Island, she likes to write about this beautiful locale in her books. The joy of family is a recurring theme in Kristine's books, a theme that Kristine knows a lot about since she is the mother of six. As well, Kristine and her husband ran a café very similar to Plain Jane's. Unfortunately, she didn't find the experience nearly as rewarding as Jane Plainfield does!

Books by Kristine Rolofson

Don't miss any of our special offers. Write to us at the following address for information on our newest releases.

Harlequin Reader Service
U.S.: 3010 Walden Ave., P.O. Box 1325, Buffalo, NY 14269
Canadian: P.O. Box 609, Fort Erie, Ont. L2A 5X3

PLAIN JANE'S MAN
KRISTINE ROLOFSON

Harlequin Books

TORONTO • NEW YORK • LONDON
AMSTERDAM • PARIS • SYDNEY • HAMBURG
STOCKHOLM • ATHENS • TOKYO • MILAN
MADRID • WARSAW • BUDAPEST • AUCKLAND

Dedicated in loving memory of Don Rocque.
Those were good times, and Hope, Idaho,
will never be the same without you.

ISBN 0-373-25607-8

PLAIN JANE'S MAN

Copyright © 1994 by Kristine Rolofson.

Prologue

September 1963

"THEY KNOW," SHE SAID without looking at him. Instead, she hugged her knees to her chest and gazed down at the distant lake. Her long yellow hair swung forward and hid her face.

The young man stood beside her, his hands jammed into the pockets of his jeans. The early rays of sunset highlighted the Cabinet Mountain Range to the west, but he ignored the jagged rose peaks. "And?" he prompted.

"They've decided—I mean, *we've* decided I should go to that home in Spokane. I can have the baby there, and no one will ever know."

"*I'll* know." He felt as if the words were torn out of his chest. His heart burned and he looked down, half expecting to see blood running down the front of his denim work shirt, and spilling into the grass. "*You'll* know."

"But I'm only twenty, and—" She put her hands over her face.

He knew what she was going to say and didn't. "Go ahead. Say it. *I can't help you.*"

"You *can't* help me," she insisted, wiping her face with her hands. "I never expected you to. Honest. It's my fault, too." Her forehead was drawn against her bent knees, her hair brushed against one long, tanned thigh. He loved her so much. She was like no one he'd ever met before and when she'd arrived in his small town for the summer—with her brown eyes and streaky blond hair and those long legs—she'd driven almost every man in town wild. That shy smile made a man want to protect her with his life and take her with his body.

"I'm sorry," he managed to choke past the lump in his throat. "For everything."

She lifted her head and finally looked at him. "I'm not. Despite everything, I will never be sorry for this summer. Or for what happened between us. We fell in love." Her smile was wry. "Despite the guilt—and I'm *loaded* with guilt—I loved you. And I'll never forget what we had together."

"How could you forget, when it's going to ruin your life? When *I've* already ruined your life?"

She scrambled to her feet and put gentle fingers on his arm. "I refuse to think of it like that." She looked past him, down to where the huge lake lay at the bottom of the mountain on which they stood. "After I've had the baby—" She cleared her throat. "After this winter, I'll go back to school. Get my degree. Become a famous artist." She looked up into his eyes and smiled. "Don't hate yourself for what happened, my love."

"That's impossible." He'd known all along, right from the beginning, that he'd never be able to give her what she deserved. "I don't know why you don't hate me."

"Because I love you. *Loved* you," she amended. "You have to go back to your life, and I'll go on with mine."

"And . . . the child?"

They stood together in silence for a long moment, until she said, "The child will be fine. I'll do what's best for it—I promise."

"I don't have any other choice but to believe you. I have no right to expect anything more than that."

"Something good will come of all this," she murmured, resting her cheek against his shoulder. "It has to, because we never meant to hurt anyone."

"I should be comforting you," he said. "Instead, you're the one trying to help me."

"Please, just hold me one more time," she asked, her words muffled with tears.

They stood together on the mountainside, two lone figures in the midst of the faded remnants of summer's yellow bear grass. He held on to her as tightly as he dared, silently promising himself—and her—that he would do something to make it up to her. No matter how long it took or how impossible it seemed, he would find a way to make it right.

1

July 1994

"NUMBER ONE THIRTY-THREE!"

Jane didn't have to look at the ticket stub in her pocket to know that wasn't her number. She'd bet her last pound of ground sirloin that all of the two hundred people who'd bought a ticket to the Second Annual Bodacious Barbecue had memorized the number printed across the top. Sixty-four, the number on her ticket, was still in the running for the grand prize.

"Remember, folks," the announcer cautioned. "Now that we're down to the last fifty balls, we're going to take a thirty-minute break." There was good-natured catcalling from members of the audience in front of the stage. Roger Cantrell, mayor of East Hope, Idaho, chuckled and made the microphone squawk. "You don't begrudge me the chance to have a beer and a dance with my wife, do you? The band's going to play, you all can do a little dancin'. I'll be back in a little while, and we'll get ready to give away that brand-new Baysider boat parked over there." He pointed across the lawn. "So all you folks who haven't had their numbers called yet better make a wish or say your prayers or whatever you want to do, because before the sun sets tonight, we're going to give away that new boat!"

The crowd cheered, and Jane turned away from the stage and strolled across the lawn toward one of the makeshift bars. The relentless July sun provided a perfect day for Hope, Idaho's, annual fund-raiser, but a stronger breeze from the lake would be welcome. A trickle of perspiration snaked between her breasts and settled into the sashed waist of her white sundress.

"Hey, P.J., how's it goin'?"

"Hi, Tim," she said to the young bartender. "I'm still in the running. What about you?"

"I couldn't afford the hundred bucks for a ticket, so I volunteered to work instead. You want a gin and tonic?"

"As long as it's light on the gin. I'm not much of a drinker." She watched Tim, her best mechanic, reach into the cooler at his feet. "I didn't know bartending was one of your talents. Besides driving my waitresses into a frenzy, that is." All he had to do was walk in the door and silverware crashed to the floor.

He grinned, showing a set of perfectly matched white teeth. "You think the only thing I'm good at is fixing boats?"

"I'm not going to answer that one. How's the ice holding up?"

He tossed a handful of cubes into a plastic glass and reached for the gin. "It should last, but the way this crowd is drinking, I can't be sure."

"Let me know when you need more and I'll go back to the café and get some." She looked around as the band opened with a rendition of "All My Exes Live in Texas" and saw the dance floor fill up. "It could be a long evening."

"Maybe you'll get lucky and win the boat." He handed her the drink.

"Thanks," she said, taking a long sip. "I've never won anything in my life and besides, the last thing I need right now is a boat."

"How about a date?" He winked at her. "You don't have too many of those, especially since you keep turning me down."

Jane grinned back at the familiar request. If she were ten years younger—and a lot less wise—she'd give Tim a chance. But she'd learned the hard way what kind of trouble could result from imagining herself in love. "I'm old enough to be your, uh, sister."

"Give me a break. I like older women."

"Ouch!" She made a face, knowing he wasn't serious. He'd teased her about her age since she'd turned thirty a few months ago.

"So do I," a male voice said behind her. She turned around to see an attractive, dark-haired man. "But I don't think you qualify."

"Probably not," she replied, although he didn't look as if he could be much older than she was. "Unless you're under thirty, I'm old enough to be your sister, too." Who was he? Someone's guest, no doubt, because she knew everyone in town. Thirty-two, she guessed, with a very unmarried twinkle in his brown eyes.

"I don't have any sisters," he answered on a sigh. "Never wanted any." He turned to the grinning bartender. "Scotch and soda, please."

"Coming right up."

Jane moved sideways, but the stranger stopped her. "I'm thirty-five. Thought you should know, so when I ask you to dance you have enough information."

"I thought you liked older women."

He accepted his drink from Tim and thanked him, without taking his gaze from Jane. "But you haven't told me how old you are. I can't believe you're over thirty."

"Not 'over.' I just celebrated that milestone a few months ago."

They moved out of the way as an elderly couple approached the bar. "I like younger women, too," he informed her, his lips turning up into an easy smile. He looked like the kind of man who smiled often.

Her curiosity got the better of her. "You're not from around here, are you?"

"No, I'm from Boise."

"You came up to fish?"

"Not really. It's a combination of business and pleasure. I'm staying at a resort across the bay, in East Hope." He pointed across the bay toward the towns nestled against a backdrop of rugged mountains. The tiny communities of Hope and East Hope sat side by side, facing a panoramic view of Lake Pend Oreille and the Cabinet Mountains. "The owner of the Rainbow Resort is an old friend of mine."

"Don Stone?"

"You know him?"

"Sure. One pancake, two eggs over easy, and black coffee." Her companion looked blank, so Jane explained, "I own the café next to the Rainbow. Don comes over for breakfast every morning."

The man's brown eyes twinkled. "And the young bartender? What does he order?"

"English muffin, with ham and cheese inside. To go."

He held her gaze with an appreciative one of his own. Jane decided she was having a pretty good time. After all, she was accustomed to making conversation with people. That's what her customers expected when they walked into her café: a little conversation, something to eat and the latest gossip with the neighbors.

He looked around and pointed to the mayor, who danced past them doing the two-step with a silver-haired woman. "What about him?"

"Roger? Ham, eggs, home fries and a large glass of milk."

He took another swallow of his drink, then nodded toward a very tall man in jeans and a T-shirt that read, It Takes a Stud to Build a House. "Don't tell me you feed him, too."

"That's Cliff. Grilled cheese and ham, side order of onion rings."

He grimaced. "Onion rings for breakfast?"

"He likes them."

"Let's see," he drawled, looking around at the crowd that milled across the neatly clipped lawn of the Red Fir Resort. "What about that man clearing tables?"

She shook her head. "His wife cooks his breakfast, but they come to the café for dinner on Fridays, Seafood Night."

"You could be making this all up."

"Come in for breakfast some morning and see for yourself."

"All right. What do you think I'll order?"

She pretended to give the question a great deal of thought while he stood there, his twinkling eyes looking down at her as if he thought the discussion was the most interesting thing he'd heard all day. "You could be a yogurt-and-granola kind of guy," she guessed. "But I think you're an omelet man."

"Maybe I'm not that complicated."

"Then I'm wrong?"

"No," he said. "Mexican omelets are my favorite. I didn't know I was so transparent."

He looked so disgusted with himself that Jane threw her head back and laughed, which she knew she shouldn't. Her laugh could make crows flee from telephone wires. She heard someone nearby say, "There goes P.J. again!"

"Do you have a date for this?"

"No, but—"

"Neither do I. I know three people here, and they're tired of talking to me. Would you mind dancing with an omelet man?"

"It's a little hot . . . ."

"No one else thinks so," he countered. He took her hand and she surprised herself by letting him lead her to the dance floor. He stopped at one of the tables to leave their drinks.

"Look," she protested, as he swung her into his arms for a country waltz. "It's really too hot for this." But she might as well have been talking to the little alligator appliqué on his black shirt for all the good it did. He was average height—maybe five-eleven—but reaching his shoulder was still a stretch for someone who barely made it to five foot two. He was warm, but the heat seeping through her palm wasn't uncomfortable, simply the satisfying warmth of touching another human being—something she hadn't done in a very long time.

While she normally enjoyed being single, independent and accountable to no one, today she'd felt just a little bit lost, although she wouldn't have admitted it to anyone but herself.

"I heard someone call you P.J.," the man holding her said. "Is that some kind of nickname?"

"It stands for Plain Jane. That's the name of my restaurant," she explained, hoping she could dance and talk at the same time. He guided her easily through the crowd, though, and she began to relax. "Plain Jane's Café."

He chuckled in a low rumble near her ear. "Where'd you come up with a name like that?"

"It's easy to remember, which is important for a restaurant."

He looked down at her, his dark eyes flashing with good humor. "And *you're* 'Plain Jane'?"

She nodded. "And who are you?"

The music stopped, and although he released his arm from her waist, he continued to hold her hand. "Peter."

"Nice to meet you." "Nice" didn't quite cover the feeling of meeting a good-looking single man in a town of two hundred and eighty-five people, many of them over seventy. She wondered if the hot sun had caused her to hallucinate. "Who *are* you?"

"What do you mean?" He led her over to the canopied table where they'd set their drinks, but the glasses were gone. "Looks like we head back to the bar."

"I'm not much of a drinker."

"Neither am I, but I'm not used to dancing in the middle of the afternoon, either. Come on."

One of her waitresses gave her a thumbs-up sign, while two of her lunch customers grinned and waved. They passed a group of fishermen and their wives, and one of the older men looked at Peter and back to Jane and winked. Jane felt her cheeks grow pink. "Could you let go of my hand, please?"

Peter looked at their clasped hands as if he'd forgotten they were joined. "Sorry," he said, releasing her. "I didn't realize I was still holding on to you."

"Well, people are staring."

Clearly bewildered, he glanced around the gathering. "Like who?"

"Practically everyone in town. I'll never hear the end of it tomorrow morning. *P.J. found herself a boyfriend yesterday. Picked him up at the Bodacious Barbecue, saw it with my own eyes.*" She returned to a normal voice. "The fishermen will tease me all week."

"So you don't date often," he stated.

Great. Now she appeared pathetic and lonely. "I'm divorced, and this is a small town. Whenever I go out with someone people automatically think I'm going to marry him and have the wedding reception at the café."

He chuckled again. "And that's not the case?"

"No." She could have elaborated, could have said, *I like my life just the way it is, without any complications, without having to answer to anyone.* But you didn't say something like that to a total stranger, especially a summer tourist. You didn't talk about how your ex-husband married you because he wanted your father's marina and the divorce had made you a little paranoid. "What about you?"

"I've never been married," he admitted, steering her toward Tim's bar. "Never even came close. What would you like to drink?"

"Just some ice water."

"And a beer," he told Tim, who quickly filled their order.

"Good luck, P.J.," the young man said. "They're going to start to pick numbers again." He wiped his brow. "Boy, I'll be glad when this is over and I can get out of this sun."

"It's almost six," she told him. "This can't last much longer."

"Well, I hope you win."

Jane shook her head. "I told you, I've never won anything before in my life. Except a turkey from Hope School that only had one drumstick, so it tipped over sideways in the pan."

"There's champagne for the winner," Tim informed her, ignoring Peter's laughter. "Don't forget."

Peter took her arm and steered her back toward the stage where the mayor stood adjusting the microphone. "You never know, Jane," he said. "This could be your lucky day."

"What about you? Have they already called your number?"

"I have a guest ticket," he said. "I don't need a boat, either." They stood with the crowd as the drummer began a dramatic drumroll and Roger announced the resumption of the drawing.

"Don't forget, folks," he called. "We're down to the last fifty Ping-Pong balls. We're going to keep picking until there's only one left. And if the number matches the one on your ticket, then you've won yourself a boat. Now, let's get started!"

"Do you want to sit down?" Peter whispered in her ear.

"I'm fine."

"Do you know everyone here?"

"Almost, although there are a lot of people who are probably from Sandpoint." She added, "That's a larger town about fifteen miles south of here."

"How far away is Spokane?"

"A hundred miles."

"Fifty-two! Who has fifty-two?"

Peter leaned closer. "What's your number?"

"Sixty-four," she murmured. "Which is also the year I was born, so it's easy to remember."

"One ninety-nine!" A loud groan came from underneath one of the tents. Roger looked toward the sound. "Marge Baker, is that you? You didn't win the boat, but you've won yourself a nice bottle of wine from our local vineyard. Come on up and get it!"

The crowd cheered.

"Obviously a local person," Peter said.

"She works at the Hi Hopes Market."

They stood side by side in the crowd as the countdown continued. "You're still in the running," Peter said, sounding impressed.

"I can't believe it." The prizes included bottles of wine, dinners at local restaurants, such as Plain Jane's Café, and gift certificates for stores in Sandpoint.

"We're down to the final ten," the mayor crowed. "So we're going to take another short break, to build the suspense, and then I'm going to ask those of you whose number hasn't been called yet to come onstage."

"Onstage?"

Peter turned to look at her. "Don't look so depressed. You have a one-in-ten chance to win a Baysider boat."

"I don't want it."

Surprise crossed his face. "What did you say?"

"I don't want it," she repeated. "My father and I own a marina."

"So you already have a boat," he said, looking relieved. She couldn't figure out why he'd care.

"No. My father does, but I don't—"

"P.J.!" Roger waved to her and hurried over. "We sure appreciated the ice you donated. I didn't think we'd need that much, though. Hope we didn't leave the restaurant short."

"We'll be fine. There's a delivery tomorrow," she assured him. "It was a lot hotter this year."

Roger turned to Peter. "I'm Roger Cantrell."

Jane started to introduce the men, but realized she didn't know Peter's last name. "Peter—"

"Johnson," he supplied.

Roger's face lit up. "From Baysider?"

"Yes."

"Well, we're sure happy you could come up here in person. We never expected it, that's for sure, but we appreciate the deal you gave us on the boat."

Jane turned to him. "Your company sells Baysider?"

"We *build* Baysider," he replied, shaking Roger's hand. "My stepmother arranged everything. She grew up around here and insisted I see this area for myself."

"I hope you're not disappointed," Roger said, with the confidence of someone who knew he lived in one of the most beautiful places in the world. He gestured toward the mountains across the lake. "We've been compared to Switzerland, you know."

"I can see why."

Jane edged away. "If you'll excuse me," she began, but Peter took her hand and held on.

"Excuse us, will you?" he said to the mayor. "I think Jane needs a little moral support. She's one of your finalists."

Roger waved them off. "Good luck, Janie! See you onstage!"

"Janie?" Peter repeated.

"He's an old friend of the family. Most everyone calls me P.J."

"I'd rather call you Jane." He tugged her toward an empty corner of the tent and didn't stop until they were in the shade. "Why don't you want to win one of my boats? I designed this particular one myself."

"I didn't mean to hurt your feelings."

"You didn't." He flashed her the charming grin once again. "At least, not much. But you have to admit, you're probably the only ticket holder here who didn't want to win."

Jane felt her cheeks grow pink. It really was a hot day. "I think I'm going to get another glass of water," she said. She wasn't about to explain to a man who built boats that she was afraid of the water.

"I'll get it for you," he offered.

"No, thanks." She took a step away, leaving the welcome shade of the tent.

"You're leaving me," he said, pretending to be disappointed. "I didn't think it would come to this so soon."

"You'll get over it eventually," she told him, unable to hide her smile.

"I don't think it will be easy," Peter answered, with mock despair. "But I have hope. If you win the boat, you'll have to see me again."

PETER STOOD IN THE shade of the yellow-striped tent and watched the tiny brunette make her way through the crowd.

Just his luck to find a woman who was born in 1964 and grew up in Hope, Idaho. He'd known he shouldn't have gotten involved in Ruth's crazy scheme, but he'd never been able to refuse his stepmother anything. She'd never asked for much, until a few months ago. He'd managed to stall her, until she'd heard about the Bodacious Barbecue fund-raiser. There'd been no peace in Boise since.

Was there a "Jane" on the list the detective had sent him? He couldn't remember. All in all, he probably didn't have much potential as a detective. Subterfuge and mysteries had never excited him. Peter finished his beer and watched the people wander across the green lawn of the resort. Someone here knew what happened that summer of 1963, and unfortunately he couldn't leave north Idaho until he'd uncovered the truth.

"WAY TO GO, P.J.!" a woman called from the crowd. "Do you feel lucky today?"

Jane grinned. "I'll let you know in a minute."

She stood on the stage with nine other people, three of whom were customers of the restaurant, and waited to hear Roger announce the first number.

"One forty-two," he called, and a robust man on Jane's right moaned.

"You've won a weekend at The Coeur d'Alene," Roger informed him. "A very nice prize."

One by one the balls were picked from their wire basket until only two remained. Jane stood on Roger's right, while a young man stood on his left.

"We're going to pick the winning number in just a second, here, folks. But first I'd like to introduce the owner of Baysider Boats, and a man who gave us a great deal on this grand prize. We really appreciate it, too, so let's give Peter Johnson a great big round of applause. Come on up here, Peter, and get ready to present the keys to the boat to our big winner here."

He really was handsome, with that charming grin and those brown eyes, Jane thought. One of those brown eyes winked at her. She bit back a laugh and turned away. She still couldn't believe she might win Peter's boat. What did a short-order cook need with an eighteen-foot boat? She didn't water-ski or fish. She couldn't give it to her father. He'd decided to do some traveling and besides, he already owned a boat—the same one he'd loved for fifteen years. Jane couldn't picture her father fishing in anything else.

"Drumroll, please," Roger said, grabbing the handle of the basket and turning it to make the balls bounce. The band played the first notes of "Row Your Boat" as Roger stuck his hand in the basket and picked out a Ping-Pong ball.

"The second-prize winner is number... *eighteen!*"

The young man groaned, then shrugged. "What'd I win?"

Roger clapped him on the shoulder. "A season pass for Schweitzer Ski Basin." He turned to Jane. "P.J., do you have your ticket stub?"

Jane pulled the paper out of her pocket. Her heart sank to her stomach. This was crazy. She would have preferred the weekend in Coeur d'Alene. How could a person who didn't like the water possibly win a boat? She tried to smile. The crowd expected it of her. Roger pulled out the last Ping-Pong ball, checked the number, and handed it to Peter. "You want to read that number, son?"

"Sixty-four," he said.

Jane handed Roger her ticket stub. "I think it's a match." Peter dangled the boat keys in front of her, while the crowd applauded. Jane took the keys, Roger hugged her, and Peter took her hand to lead her off the stage.

"Congratulations," he said.

"Thank you. And thank you for the boat. I don't know what—"

"Stay and dance, everyone!" Roger called through the microphone. "P.J.'s going to open a bottle of champagne, there's still beer in the kegs, and the band's going to play until sundown. The houseboat leaves every half hour or so to take you across the bay to your cars, so enjoy the party and drive carefully. And thank you all for making this another successful fund-raiser for our community center!"

"You could sell it," Peter suggested. "I'm sure you could get a pretty good amount of money for it."

She shook her head. "That doesn't seem right. Everyone in town wanted to win it. Turning around and putting a For Sale sign on it doesn't seem very nice."

"Would you like champagne or a cup of coffee?"

"Champagne." She looked down at their clasped hands. "I thought we said goodbye."

"I told you that you'd see me again if you won the boat. Now you're stuck with me."

"You and the boat go together?"

"I guess you could say that. Any objections?"

Jane pretended to hesitate. She'd have to be crazy to resist spending the rest of the afternoon with a handsome man—especially one with a sense of humor and the ability to dance without stepping on her feet. "No objections at all."

2

"HERE'S TO LUCK," Peter said, raising his plastic champagne glass. Jane lifted hers, surprisingly comfortable in the bucket seat facing the Baysider's steering wheel. Peter had insisted she sit in her prize, and someone from the Sandpoint *Daily Bee* had snapped a picture.

"To luck," she echoed, and sipped the bubbling liquid. "I can't help feeling guilty, though."

"About winning?"

"Yes."

"Why? You bought a ticket, just like everyone else. You were just luckier than the other one hundred and ninety-nine people."

"But—"

"No," he interrupted her. "Tonight you're going to dance with me. Tomorrow you can decide what you're going to do with this boat." He patted the dashboard. "She's a nice little boat, you know. You should give her a chance."

"I'll give it some thought." She wished she'd worn a hat. She could feel her hair frizzing in the heat. It was too late to worry about how she looked, but she hoped she looked cooler than she felt. The champagne was ice cold and pleasantly tart, so she finished her glass and held it out for more.

"Are you sure?" Peter hesitated before pouring.

"Positive. You're right. I might as well celebrate now and worry about what I'm going to do tomorrow." She didn't usually act like Scarlett O'Hara, but she decided she could blame the sudden personality change on the relentless sun. Or the shock of winning something. Or a startling reaction to a handsome stranger.

She giggled—another uncharacteristic behavior. At least it was something she could blame on the champagne.

"Are you sure you're all right?" he asked. "What about some ice water?"

"Let's dance." She finished the second glass of champagne and stood. "Can you two-step?"

"Yes," he said, standing and taking her hand as if he was afraid she'd fall out of the boat. "Nothing fancy, but I can get you around the floor."

"That's all that counts," she assured him, climbing over the railing to the wooden steps. "Since I seem to have been picked up by a handsome stranger, I guess I'd better make the most of it."

"I picked you up?"

"Well, I didn't make any moves on you." She let him lead her across the lawn toward the music.

"You smiled at me," he said. "That was all it took." He swung her into his arms. "I always like it when women do that."

"DO YOU GET THE feeling we've missed the boat?"

Jane sat down on the dock and watched the tiny waves lap against the wood. "Are you speaking mataphor—uh—metaphorically?"

"No. I'm talking about tonight." He looked down at her and frowned. "You've had way too much to drink."

"I had to celebrate. Everyone said so."

"I should have gotten some coffee into you earlier."

"Not your fault," she reassured him, hoping he could understand her words. She'd lost all feeling in her upper lip hours ago. "I wanted to dance."

"Well, we danced, all right." He sat down beside her on the dock. Above them the last of the barbecue organizers cleaned the grounds and the band dismantled their equipment.

Jane looked at the lights across the bay. "I never heard anyone say the houseboat was leaving."

"Neither did I." He took her hand. "Maybe we can get a ride with someone in the band."

"Okay." Jane attempted to stand, but couldn't move. "I think my legs have disappeared."

"It's the champagne." He stood and tried to haul her to her feet, but she collapsed into giggles and stayed where she was.

"I never do this," she admitted, catching her breath. "I get up at five-thirty every morning."

"I just want you to get up off the dock," he muttered. "I can't leave you here. You could fall in the lake and drown."

"It's really nice of you to worry."

He ran his fingers through his hair. "I'm a nice guy."

She would have liked to believe him, but even champagne couldn't renew her faith in men. "You came over by boat?"

"Yeah. Don brought me in his." He sat down beside her and put his arm over her shoulder. "Are you going to be all right?"

"Look at the moon," she said, pointing above them. "It's a perfect night."

Peter looked. "It's too bad we can't put your boat in the water and go home."

"Tree—I mean *true*." She giggled again, promising herself it would be the last time. She really had to get a grip, but she wasn't exactly sure how to do it. She'd danced, twirling in Peter's arms or rocking to the faster songs. And she'd killed off her bottle of champagne and probably someone else's, too. Her friends, neighbors and customers had been so happy for her, and she'd accepted a lot of hugs and congratulations.

All in all, it had been quite a party. Now a wide silver strip of moonlight shone on the water and the lights of Hope twinkled against the mountains. If she could fly she'd be home in five minutes. She leaned her head against Peter's sturdy shoulder. "This is nice," she managed to say.

"Yes, it is, but it's a long walk around the peninsula to get back to Hope, so we'd better—"

"I could sit here all night and look at the moon."

"I'm sure you could," he agreed, laughter edging his voice. "But I have to get us home. Where do you live, anyway?"

She pointed to the marina. "There."

"Could you be a little more specific?"

"I have a trailer, a *mobile home*, beside the café. It's very convenient."

"I'm sure it is. And if you could stand, I could take you there."

She wriggled her toes. Somewhere she'd lost her sandals. "My feet work," she assured him. "We could try again."

He got to his feet and reached for her. "Put your arms around my neck," he said, bending down. "And don't let go."

"Okay." She smoothed her hands over his shoulders, then higher. His hair was soft under her fingertips, the skin on his neck warm and smooth. Dangerously smooth. She started to lift her fingers away from his neck.

"Hang on," he ordered, so she tightened her grip. He lifted her easily to her feet, grasping her waist until she steadied herself. "All right?"

She nodded, her hands still clasped around his neck. His eyes were very dark in the shadowy night. He looked down at her and sighed. "Damn," he muttered, bending lower to touch his lips to hers. She couldn't help kissing him back, despite her numb lips. He pulled her close against him, his hands gripping her waist as if he was afraid she'd run away.

Jane closed her eyes against the moonlight and touched his hair. He moved his mouth against hers with a butterfly softness that threatened her ability to stand. She wanted to sink to the wooden dock, bringing him down with her. Instead, she hung on to his shoulders, willing herself to stay upright. God only knew what would happen in a horizontal position.

His hands seemed to burn through the thin cotton of her dress. His lips nibbled at the corner of her mouth, then across her jaw to the delicate flesh below her ear.

"You folks need a ride?"

Jane froze. "Did you just say something?"

Peter stopped, then lifted his head. "No."

"Then who did?"

"That man over there in a, uh, tugboat."

"Ed," Jane supplied, knowing the only owner of a tugboat on this part of the lake. But why would Ed be watching her kiss this man from Boise?

"If you say so."

Jane released her hold on Peter and turned to see an older man standing on the stern of a small tugboat tied up to a neighboring dock. "Hi, Ed."

"You want a ride home?" he called. "I'm goin' that way."

"Sure," Peter answered for both of them. "We missed the houseboat's last trip back."

"The *Alibi* left without you? No problem. Come on over."

Peter moved backward, taking Jane with him. Her feet didn't budge, so she swayed in his arms. "Come on," he urged.

"No."

"No?"

"I'd rather ride in a car," she whispered. "I'm sure someone will give us a ride. If we just ask."

"Yeah, but I've never ridden on a tugboat before. And it might be easier to get you on that than to climb all these stairs to the parking lot. It was hard enough to get you to stand."

"Don't remind me. I *know* I drank too much champagne, but I can still—"

"Come on," he ordered, helping her along the path to the neighboring dock. "You can tell me all about it on the way home."

Ed reached out a gnarled hand to help her aboard, and Jane prayed she wouldn't disgrace herself by falling flat on her face. Her legs just didn't seem to be very steady. The flat deck of the tug was covered with coils of rope, and there was a dark tarp folded in one corner. It smelled of gasoline and dead fish, but those were two odors Jane was accustomed to.

"Peter Johnson," Peter said, accepting Ed's offer of a hand.

"Ed Kennedy. Nice to meet you, young man." He tipped his hat. "You're not from around here?"

"No."

"He brought the keys to the boat," Jane explained. "He's an omelet man from Boise."

Ed looked back at Peter. "Had a little to drink, did she?"

Peter grinned. "You could say that. I'm just trying to get her home in one piece."

"Well, hang on to her," the old man cautioned. "Can't lose the cook." He went into the wheelhouse and within minutes the tug's engine roared to life. Peter took Jane by the shoulders and pushed her gently down onto the tarp.

"So you don't fall overboard," he explained.

"Don't joke."

He wrapped his arms around her, pleased that she snuggled into his chest. He didn't think she snuggled easily, but he probably had the champagne to thank. "Cold?"

"Yes," she admitted. "And dizzy."

"That's because I'm such a good kisser."

She giggled, making him glad she wasn't too dizzy to laugh. "You *are* a pretty good kisser," she replied. "You must practice a lot on those southern Idaho women."

He lifted her chin. "Northern Idaho women are turning out to be more interesting." He brushed his lips against hers.

"I don't usually do things like this," she whispered, her arms reaching up to wrap around his neck.

"Like what?"

"Kiss strangers."

"I didn't think I was a stranger anymore," he murmured against her mouth. Her lips were soft and warm under his, and he felt her shiver beneath his hands. He continued to kiss her as they crossed the bay. The boat moved slowly, vibrating from the nearby engine, belching clouds of smoke as it plowed through the black water.

Silence surrounded them. Peter wondered if he'd finally gone deaf from the tug's roaring engine until he heard Ed's gravelly voice.

"You two can't stay here tonight," the old man said. "Though you sure do look comfortable."

Peter reluctantly lifted his mouth from Jane's. "Come on. I think we've docked."

"Where?" Her eyes looked sleepy.

"I don't know."

He untangled himself from the tarp and helped Jane to her feet. She swayed slightly, but he managed to hang on to her.

"We're home," she said, looking at the dock. "Come on."

"Hang on."

"Okay." She climbed off the tug and landed on her knees on the wooden dock. "'Bye, Ed. See you tomorrow."

"Sure, honey. You get some rest." The old man winked, and uncoiled a fistful of rope.

"Thanks for the ride," Peter said, lifting Jane to her feet. "Point us in the right direction," he told her.

She gestured at a cluster of buildings behind the maze of wooden docks and walkways. "That way." She looked down at her dress and frowned. "I hope I didn't get dirt on it."

Peter thought of the filthy tarp they'd just sat on for the past twenty minutes. "Come on," he said, taking her hand. "You can do your laundry tomorrow."

She smiled up at him. "Okay."

They walked along the narrow boards, up the slight incline and past the gas pumps, bait house and huge red-painted shop. Jane led him toward a small mobile home parked behind a compact ranch house. "Home, thank goodness," she said. "On solid ground."

She dropped his hand and rummaged beneath a flowerpot for the key. When she tried to unlock the door, he took the key from her.

"There you go," he said, opening the door.

She managed the two steps up, then turned to him and frowned. "Hurry up. Someone might see you."

Peter wondered if that was some kind of invitation to come into her home. He looked over his shoulder at the empty parking lot, half expecting to see a crowd of curious onlookers, but except for a barking dog the area was quiet. He turned and followed her into the trailer, ducking at the last minute to avoid a serious head injury.

"Wait a sec," she cautioned. "There's a light around here somewhere." He heard her bump into something and swear softly under her breath.

"You okay?"

She switched on a tiny lamp above a table and he was able to see that they were standing in the kitchen area, beyond which lay couches and what he assumed was a bedroom. It was more spacious than he would have guessed from looking at the outside.

"I'm still a little dizzy," she admitted, turning to him with that smile that had so attracted him in the first place. It made him want to take her into his arms and watch her smile as he made love to her. "Maybe I should make some coffee."

Peter watched her hang on to the back of a chair for support. "Maybe you'd better let me do it."

"Okay." She pulled out the wooden chair and sat down. "The coffeepot is there behind you, on the counter. The coffee and the filters are in the cupboard above."

He turned and, after some searching, managed to construct a pot of coffee and flip the switch to turn on the machine. "All I could find was decaf," he announced, turning to her. Jane leaned on the tabletop, resting her head on her folded arms. Her dark curls spilled over her cheek, but he could see that her eyes were closed. "Jane?"

There was no answer, just the sizzling drip of the coffee into the glass carafe. Peter stepped over to her and touched her shoulder. "Jane," he whispered, but she didn't stir. He couldn't leave her hunched over the table like some old drunk at a bar, but he hesitated to wake her. Even if he could rouse her, what was he to do? Carry her to bed?

BUZZING RIPPED THROUGH her skull, sending waves of pain through her temples. Why was Daddy sawing logs in the middle of the night? Jane put her hands over her ears and resisted opening her eyes. She burrowed back under the covers, willing the invasive buzzing to stop.

It didn't. Gradually she realized the sound was either her alarm clock or someone was cutting her skull open. She reached behind her and fumbled for the clock, smashing the top of it with her fist until she hit the Off switch. Blessed quiet filled the room. *I am in my bed, it's morning, and I don't know why my head feels as if I've had brain surgery.*

Jane lay very still, trying to remember. Yesterday she'd won the grand prize of the barbecue, the Baysider boat. She'd met a very nice man who could two-step like a Texan. And she'd celebrated—obviously a little too much, judging from the pounding across her temples. For a woman who hardly ever drank anything stronger than diet cola, she'd managed to tie one on.

And now she had to get up and go to work. The café would open in an hour and she needed to have the grill hot and the coffee ready for the early risers. If she could only open her eyes, she'd be on her way.

It took longer than she would have thought to sit up, open her eyes and swing her legs over the edge of the bed. She looked down at the sundress bunched around her waist. She smelled gasoline, and there were suspicious dark spots on the hem of her once-white, once-new dress. Not only must she have gone to bed with her clothes on, but she'd rolled around in an engine room first.

She moaned, leaning forward, as the memories of kissing a tall, handsome man came back to her. Peter Somebody, from Boise. And hitching a ride on the Kennedy tugboat. After that, everything was a blank.

Jane got out of the bed and slid open her bedroom door. The good news was that she still had her clothes on. The bad news, she realized, staring into the living room, was that the man from Boise was asleep on her couch.

She tiptoed up to him and peered down. Flat on his back, his arms thrown over his head, he snored softly. An appealing masculine stubble covered his chin, and his dark hair lay mussed across his forehead. Definitely the kind of man who looked good "the morning after," although—thank goodness—there'd been no "night before." She'd been alone since her divorce, which was safer for lots of reasons. But Peter from Boise could tempt a saint, and she remembered the twinkle in those dark eyes.

What was she going to do with him? It was almost six, and she couldn't just leave him here. What if someone saw him leave her house this morning? In thirty minutes the parking lot would become a constant parade of trucks and cars, and anyone could see Peter step out her door and return to wherever he came from.

Female vanity won out. Jane looked down at her dirty, rumpled dress and only imagined what the rest of her looked like. She'd shower and change and get the heck out of here. Peter from Boise would just have to take care of himself. She could only hope he'd be inconspicuous when he did it.

"THREE OVER EASY and two slices of ham," Denise said, slipping the written order to the hood of the grill over Jane's head.

Jane pushed her baseball cap back. "It's going to take a few minutes. I'm moving slowly this morning."

"No one's noticed."

"Well, keep the coffee coming and tell the boys from the railroad their hotcakes are coming up next."

"Okay." Denise looked at her boss and best friend again. "You feelin' okay? You look a little green."

Jane shook her head. "I could use a couple of aspirin, when you get a chance." She flipped the hotcakes with practiced ease.

"Comin' right up," Denise said. She looked younger than thirty-two, with her yellow hair tied in a ponytail. "If anything happens to you, I'll have to get behind that grill and you *know* what happened last time."

Jane chuckled. "The guys didn't quit teasing you for weeks."

Denise found the bottle of aspirin, then poured a glass of water. "Here. Take these and— Holy mackerel, who's that?"

Jane took the tablets and swallowed them with the water. "Who?"

"Him."

Jane looked over her shoulder in time to see last night's dancing partner heading toward the counter. She turned back to the grill, flipped the hotcakes onto plates and handed them to Denise. "Here. This should keep them happy."

"Good morning, Jane," a familiar voice said. Jane braced herself and turned around. Several pairs of curious eyes watched her for a reaction.

"Good morning." Peter slid onto the empty stool at the end of the counter. Any closer and he'd be frying on the grill. If he mentioned spending the night in her trailer she'd dip him in batter and cook him herself. If the fishermen caught wind of that, she'd never hear the end of it. Gossipy as a bunch of crows, they'd make her life miserable with their teasing.

"Coffee?" Denise paused in front of him.

"Sure." She filled a thick white mug. "Thanks," he said. "I need this."

Jane rolled her eyes and dumped another load of sliced potatoes on the grill. She heard Denise close behind her.

"Breakfast specials are posted up there, above the sink, and P.J. can make anything else you'd like."

Jane dared a glance at him as Peter took a sip of his coffee and grinned back. She returned to her work, taking the scraper to clean the grill before cracking Jim Patrick's eggs onto it.

"I'll have an omelet," he said, laughter in his voice. "Jane knows how I like it."

"She does? Since when?"

"Never mind," Jane said, flipping the eggs onto a plate and handing it to her. "Wheat toast, three slices. Should pop up any sec." Jane turned to Peter and wiped her hands on the front of her heavy white apron. "Now, what kind of omelet do you want?"

"Isn't that your dancin' partner, P.J.?" one of the men three stools down called. "You'd better feed him, 'cuz he wore himself out last night."

"Watch out, Charlie, or I'll tell your wife that you're putting butter on your hotcakes and drinking real coffee."

"I ain't gonna say another word, honey," Charlie promised. "Denise, want to bring that pot over here one more time?"

"Help yourself. I'm butterin' toast."

Peter's voice was low. "Put anything inside an omelet and I'll eat it, all right? White toast and hash browns, too." He grinned again. "I'm starving. I overslept."

Don't say where you slept. She shook her head slightly. The lift of his eyebrows was the only indication he'd gotten the message.

He raised his voice, adopting a casual tone. "Have you had a chance to look at your new boat yet?"

"No. I've been here since six. Tim's going to move it over here for me sometime today."

"Good. I can show you how it works."

She backed up slightly. "I know how it works," she replied, trying not to sound defensive. "I own a marina, remember?"

He didn't appear offended. "But you don't sell my boats. And since this is a new design, you'd better know some of its features."

"That's right," Roger said, approaching the cash register with his receipt in his hand. "It wouldn't hurt to know what you won, P.J."

Jane picked up a medium-size stainless-steel bowl. "I'll fix the man's breakfast first, okay?"

Peter chuckled. "You won't get any argument from me."

Jane turned away, reaching for the eggs. Somehow she doubted his words. The man liked to voice his opinions—that she was sure of. But she had no intention of going out on the lake in that boat. A tugboat ride in the bay, when champagne coated her fear, was one thing; willingly cruising the lake as if she intended to keep the damn boat was something else altogether.

"Do you sell fishing licenses here?"

Jane nodded, swishing the broken eggs with a fork. "You plan on doing some fishing while you're here?"

"Yes. Among other things."

"Like what?" Now she felt more comfortable, doing what she did best, chatting with the customers and breaking eggs.

She felt him hesitate, and turned in his direction with the bowl still in her hand and waited for his answer. Somehow she knew it wouldn't be truthful.

"Well," he drawled, his dark eyes sparkling, "I have to teach you how to fish in a Baysider."

"I don't fish."

"You need to learn."

"I don't think so." She turned back to the grill and poured the eggs on an open area. Then she opened the refrigerator beneath the counter and pulled out the containers of chopped vegetables.

"No time?"

"P.J. doesn't fish," Charlie volunteered. The man on his left, squeezed into the corner by the coffeemaker, agreed.

"She doesn't go out past the bay—at least, not since I've known her."

"Her father plumb gave up," the old fisherman said. "Where are you from, young man?"

"Boise."

"You've never met Chet Plainfield?"

"No. I've heard the name, though."

"Fine man." He turned back to Jane and raised his voice. "When's your dad coming back to town?"

Jane shrugged. "Whenever he feels like it, I guess. That's one of the benefits of being retired."

"I'd rather fish," Charlie muttered. "Better than traipsin' all over the damn country."

Jane privately agreed with the old fisherman. She missed her father's company, but she couldn't complain. He'd worked all his life to put food on the table; she couldn't begrudge him his first vacation. Between Denise and Tim, she'd managed to survive her first summer running the whole show, but she didn't want to do it the rest of her life.

"Where is he?" Peter asked, setting his coffee mug on the counter.

"Visiting relatives in Alaska."

"Do you have any other family?"

"An ex-husband, that's all." She layered the vegetables onto the circle of cooked eggs and carefully folded it to make a crescent. "Did you say wheat or white?"

"White. Please."

Denise slid behind the counter and reached for the coffeepot. "Any takers?" she called.

Jane winced. The noise level had increased the pain in her temples, reminding her of her shameless behavior last night. She'd like to forget it ever happened, but a Baysider lay across the bay waiting for her to claim it. And the biggest reminder sat behind the counter, less than three feet away, waiting for his breakfast.

It was going to be one hell of a day.

3

THE CAFÉ WAS A LARGE, open room. The six people who sat on the counter stools could watch their eggs being fried or their sandwiches assembled. It was the kind of place where everyone inside turned to see who came through the door each time the tiny bell rang. The kind of place where the waitress knew you by name and the cook knew you liked your burgers rare and your fries crispy.

The coffee was always hot and there was usually a neighbor to talk to. If Charlie Butler hadn't shown up to dig your new septic system, you could catch him over breakfast, buy him a cup of coffee and talk business. You could charter a boat for those cousins of your wife's, see the twenty-two-pound rainbow trout that Keith Dickerson caught this morning or find out what happened at last night's town council meeting.

All in all, it was a pretty good place to spend an hour. More, if you were retired and fishing season was over. Less if it was derby week and the fish were biting.

"Have a good time last night?" Don Stone slid onto the recently vacated stool beside Peter and nodded toward Denise.

"Hey," Peter said, turning to face one of his father's best friends. He ignored the question. "I thought I'd meet up with you here."

"I eat here every morning. Thanks," he said, as Denise placed a hot cup of coffee in front of him. "Pass that sugar bowl over here."

Peter did as he was told, hoping Don would drink his coffee and forget that his houseguest hadn't come home last night. He especially hoped he wouldn't mention it in too loud a voice. Jane had given him dagger looks since he'd walked in, which wasn't exactly the way he'd hoped to be greeted. She'd acted as if he'd come to the café to ruin her life, instead of for some decent food to fill his growling stomach.

"The usual?" Denise waited, her pencil poised over her order pad.

"Sure." He raised his voice as Jane turned around. "Hi, P.J. Congratulations on winning the boat, honey. I'm sure glad someone local got it."

"Thanks, Don."

Peter pushed his empty plate away. "I'm going to take her out later and show her how it works."

Jane ignored him, he noticed, and he hid a smile. She certainly wasn't going to make this easy. Why on earth wouldn't she consent to a simple boat ride?

"One hotcake and one egg coming up," she said, turning back to the grill.

"Don't mess with the cook," Don said under his breath.

"I'm not messing with anybody," Peter replied, keeping his voice down. He hoped the clattering noise of the restaurant hid his words. "Ruth sent me here, but I never expected—"

"She called," Don interjected. "I told her you were still asleep and that you'd call back as soon as you got up."

"She believed that?" He'd never slept past seven o'clock in his life.

"No. She told me to find you and tell you that she wanted a report." Denise placed his breakfast in front of him. "Thanks." There was a moment's reprieve while Don poured syrup over the pancake and cut up his egg, but he quickly returned to the subject of the conversation. "You going to tell me what's going on?"

"Not here."

Don nodded. "Fair enough. But whatever it is, Ruth isn't going to leave you alone until she's had her way. I've always liked the woman, but I've managed to stay on her good side."

Peter thought of his tiny stepmother and shuddered. He'd worshiped her since he was fourteen, when she'd married his father and turned a somber house into a loving and happy home. But she was the most stubborn woman he'd ever met. At least, he thought, watching Jane scrape the grill, until now. "So have I. Or at least, I've tried."

"You're all she's got. And you can do no wrong," Don pronounced, spearing a large portion of pancake.

Peter thought of the enormous job she'd given him to accomplish, and how much it meant to her. "Well," he said, picking up his coffee cup, "let's hope she continues to feel that way. She's not going to be happy until I've done what she's wanted me to do."

Don grinned. "Aren't all women like that?"

Jane hovered nearby with the coffeepot. "Like what?"

Peter wished she wasn't wearing that thick shapeless apron. He remembered those soft curves beneath his palms.

"Dancing fools," he replied, trying to stick pins in her impersonal treatment of him. After all, they'd necked on a tugboat last night. She could at least smile at him this morning. "Women like to dance."

Her cheeks flushed with pink and she turned to Don and refilled his cup. "This man is a friend of yours?"

Don nodded. "I knew his father, and I've known Peter since the day he was born."

"Does he ever take no for an answer?"

Peter chuckled and shook his head, but Don hesitated before answering. "The boy has always known what he wants."

Jane removed Peter's empty plate and walked over to the sink, leaving him with a view of her cute little bottom ten feet away. He tried not to be obvious, but the woman had a body on her, that was for sure. An elbow in his ribs distracted him from the view at the sink.

"C'mon, kid. Let's take a walk." Don stood and tossed some bills on the table. He shook his head when Peter reached for his wallet. "It's on me," he insisted.

"No," Jane said, stepping back to the counter. She pushed Don's money toward him. "I owe Peter breakfast."

Charlie leaned forward. "You do?"

She ignored him, as Don picked up the bills and replaced them in his wallet. "He got me home safely. I appreciate it," she said, turning to Peter.

"So now we're even?"

She smiled, and his stomach tightened. "That's right."

Peter shook his head. "No, not quite. You owe me the chance to show you my boat. I'll be back later."

DENISE WIPED HER HANDS on a checked dish towel and turned to Jane. "You going to tell me about it?"

"There's nothing to tell."

"Yeah, and I'm a natural blonde," the waitress snorted. "You've had a guilty look on your face since he walked in."

There was no need to ask who "he" was. She'd known Denise since she was eleven. "I'm not feeling guilty about anything."

Denise shook her head. "You took him home last night, didn't you? I can't believe you—"

"Shh!" She grabbed her arm and hauled her into the supply room. "I didn't. Not exactly."

Her blue eyes narrowed. "What do you mean, 'Not exactly'?"

"I had a little too much to drink. We missed the *Alibi*'s last trip across the bay, and ended up on Ed Kennedy's tugboat."

"*You* went out on the lake?"

"Just across the bay. I've done that before, and at least this time I'd had enough champagne not to care too much."

"The last time I saw you, you were drinking water and dancing with this Peter Johnson, the boatbuilder guy. You looked perfectly normal."

"That was before I won the boat." Jane closed her eyes for one brief, heavenly moment. She only hoped she'd live through this day. "Things got a little crazy after that."

"Obviously."

"Can a man get a cup of coffee around here?" a male voice called.

Denise stuck her head out the door and hollered, "For heaven's sake, help yourself! You know where the cups are, Corky. Can't a woman get a break around here?"

"Sorry," the man muttered, and Denise popped back into the storage room. Jane leaned her forehead against a bag of flour and prayed for peace and quiet.

"You don't look so good, hon."

"I don't usually drink. My head feels like it's been hit with a splitting maul."

"Tell me about Peter."

"We danced."

"And?"

"We, uh, did some kissing on the dock."

"And?"

"I don't remember much after the tugboat."

Denise patted her on the back. "Here's the big question. Was he in your trailer this morning?"

Jane kept her eyes closed and nodded.

"He *was?* Oh, my God, P.J., I can't believe—"

"Be quiet, please, or my head could split apart. I will never drink champagne again."

"Sorry."

"He wasn't in bed with me. He slept on the couch. He was there when I woke up, so I left him. I just hope no one saw him leave the trailer."

"It wouldn't be the scandal of the century, but it would be close," Denise agreed. "Cheer up. It just proves you're human."

Jane turned around and leaned on the wall of shelves. She opened her eyes and squinted at her friend. "What's that supposed to mean?"

"Well—" Denise chuckled "—you haven't let a man near you since you kicked your ex-husband out of town, and every single guy around here has tried to ask you out."

"That's not true."

"They've all thought about it, I know that much." Denise met Jane's gaze. "More than one has asked my advice."

"And what did you say?"

"Depends on who it was. Most of the time I just told them to go ahead and ask you out and see what happened." She readjusted her ponytail and took a lipstick from her purse on the shelf. "I knew you'd say no, but you're better at hurting people's feelings than I am."

"If I could understand what you just said, I think *my* feelings would be hurt."

"Nonsense." Denise finished applying a coat of rose lipstick before tossing it back into her purse. "People are used to you. You can say just about anything and get away with it. I have to be nicer. I'm a mother."

Jane closed her eyes again, wishing she was anything but a short-order cook with a boat and a hangover.

"Anybody cooking breakfast around here today?" another male voice called.

"You're taking your life in your hands," another man warned. "They're both in the closet, yakkin'."

Jane smoothed her apron and grinned at her friend. "Guess we have to go back to work."

Denise rolled her eyes. "Men! Can't leave 'em alone for two minutes."

Jane looked at her watch. "We should get a break pretty soon."

"Not soon enough."

Jane followed her friend out of the storeroom and took her place behind the grill. No matter what had happened yesterday, she had customers to feed this morning. It was time to get her mind back on business. And off the memory of Peter's twinkling brown eyes.

"I'VE BEEN HERE less than twenty-four hours, Ruth," Peter explained. He looked at the list of names sitting in his opened briefcase. "No," he fibbed. "There hasn't been time to contact the detective." He paused. "Yes, I know how much he costs. I'll get the list first thing in the morning, and if I find out anything I'll let you know." He paused again, letting Ruth get in the last word.

"Watch your blood pressure," he teased. "I'm taking care of everything." After another minute of her instructions, Peter said goodbye and hung up the phone. He looked out the window at the lake glistening in the morning sun. Don had relented, letting him move out of the house and into a cabin, for which Peter insisted on paying.

He didn't know how long he'd have to stay in Hope, and he didn't want to take advantage of Don's hospitality. The two-room cabins that made up the Rainbow Resort sat to the west of the main house and faced the lake and the mountain range beyond. Large fir trees and a high redwood fence ensured their privacy from the main road that ran along the lakefront on its way between Montana and Washington states.

All in all, it was a great place for a vacation, even if he had to solve a mystery while he was here. And now there was more to his visit. Jane Plainfield, his reluctant dancing partner, was going to figure in his plans. Whether she liked it or not.

He'd liked dancing with her, and he'd liked kissing her. He'd certainly liked their passionate tugboat ride.

All he had to do now was convince her that she liked him, too, that there could be more to their relationship than an impersonal Mexican omelet.

He picked up the list and read it over again. Eighteen names, with Jane Plainfield's right there at the bottom. All babies conceived in the summer of 1963, born in Spokane in the spring of 1964 and adopted into waiting families.

He didn't know how the detective had found these names, especially since Potter House had been closed for years and no longer took in pregnant girls. Well, that's what Ruth paid good money for.

"Can I come in?"

Peter looked at Don standing behind the screen door. "Yeah. I just finished talking with Ruth."

Don entered the tiny pine-paneled living area. "You going to be comfortable here? If not, the house is always available."

"I'm fine. I'm glad you had the cancellation."

Don shrugged. He looked at the paper in Peter's hand. "That part of the reason you're here?"

Peter nodded. "A few months ago Ruth's sister died, the last one in the family. The whole family grew up between here and Clark Fork, across from the slough."

"The Parkinses."

"Yes. Ruth came across a lot of old letters, and found out that her brother Mitch, the one who drowned on the lake in 1963, could have fathered an illegitimate child that summer. He was in love with a summer vis-

itor, who was pregnant and supposedly went to Spokane to have the baby."

"How much of this is true?"

"I don't know. We're talking about rumors that are
over thirty years old. Ruth wouldn't leave me alone
until I came up here to find out what happened to the
child."

"A child who would be thirty now."

"And Ruth's only brother's child." He tossed the list
back into the briefcase and snapped it shut. "Enough
of that," he said, his frown turning to a smile. His stepmother's list could wait until tomorrow. For now, visions of his independent dancing partner filled his
thoughts. "Tell me about Jane Plainfield. Does she go
out with anyone special around here?"

"YOU DIDN'T HAVE TO wait here for me."

Jane turned around. Peter guided her new Baysider
neatly against the dock, near the gas pumps, and tossed
the rope onto the wooden planks. She grabbed it automatically and tied it to the metal hook nearby. "I
wasn't—" She saw his grin and realized he was teasing,
and she'd been trapped into replying. "What do you
want?"

"I brought your prize," he stated, waving one arm.
"Tim and I put it in the water, and now I'm gassing it
up for you."

She walked over to the gas pumps and unhooked one
of the nozzles.

"I'll do that," he said, climbing out of the boat.

"That's okay. I grew up doing this job."

"Why aren't you frying hamburgers?"

"I close at five on Sundays," she said, allowing him to take the nozzle from her grasp and start filling the tank. Suddenly she was glad she'd had time to change out of her cooking clothes and into clean denim shorts and a yellow T-shirt. At least she didn't smell like French fries anymore. Or she hoped she didn't. She'd showered and washed her hair, but she still worried.

"Good. You can have dinner with me." He didn't give her a chance to argue. "I've packed a picnic."

"A picnic?"

"I told you I'd be back. You probably don't need much of a lesson in operating a boat," he admitted, "but I needed the excuse to see you again."

She told herself she shouldn't feel warmed by his words. The summer sun, soon to set behind the mountains, was still bright and heating her face, that was all. And she was too old to fall for a smooth line and a charming smile.

He finished filling the tank and hooked it back on the side of the pump. "You're not going to say no again, are you?"

Then again, maybe she wasn't too old. The hopeful expression in his dark eyes was hard to resist. It was too easy to remember the way his mouth fit against hers. She had to be careful, she reminded herself. She couldn't let passion overrule years of good judgment. She looked away from Peter toward the boat. "I guess I haven't much choice, do I?"

He winced. "You're going to hurt my feelings if you keep talking like that."

"Sorry. I think you should know—"

"You have a boyfriend who's a professional wrestler with a jealous streak?"

"Worse."

His eyebrows rose. "How much worse?"

"I don't like the water."

Peter didn't look convinced. "You were on a tugboat last night."

"The champagne numbed my fear."

"Why don't you like boats?"

"I fell out of a boat when I was four. There was a bad storm, and my father had taken me fishing with him. Luckily I had my life jacket on, or I would have drowned."

"You don't go out on the lake at all?"

She shook her head. "Just the bay," she replied. "Where I'm protected from the rough water." She waited for him to laugh. After all, what could be funnier than a marina owner who wouldn't go out on the lake?

"All right," he conceded. "We'll stay in the shelter of the bay. It's plenty big enough for our purposes, anyway. And we'll stay within twenty feet of shore, if that will make you feel more comfortable."

"It would." Still, she hesitated, until he took her hand and helped her into the boat. He held on to her and untied the rope with one hand, then pushed away from the dock.

"Here," he said, leading her toward the steering wheel. He pointed to the key. "Start her up."

She did as she was told, feeling the engine roar to life. It was second nature to guide the boat away from the shore, point west and begin a slow cruise around the periphery of Ellisport Bay. Peter explained the various controls on the panel until, satisfied she'd learned the basics, Jane relinquished her place at the wheel.

They slowly passed the Red Fir Resort, where the yellow tents still stood on the top of the hill. Several people waved from the dock, and Jane waved back. Sitting on a dock dangling her feet in the water was her idea of a good time. She wished she could trade places with the resort's guests.

When the boat neared the open water, Peter slowed the engine to a crawl. "Did you bring a fishing license?"

"No." She'd left her wallet locked in the house while she'd gone to the dock to check up on the high school kid she'd hired to pump gas on weekends.

"Too bad. Don gave me some poles to use."

"I think you have to be out in deep water to troll for anything big," she told him. "Feel free to take the boat out tomorrow and try your luck."

"Thanks, but don't you have the afternoon off tomorrow?"

"How did you know that?"

"Denise told me."

"What does that have to do with the boat?"

"You may want to use it."

"No, I don't think so."

"Are you going to name her?"

"I don't know what I'm going to do with her. It doesn't seem right to sell it, after everyone else in town hoped to win her, but I don't know what else to do."

"You can keep her. Just for the rest of the summer." He didn't know why it was so important that she hang on to the boat, but it was the only link he had with her—for now—and if she sold the boat he'd have no excuse to be with her.

Except for the list. And he wasn't going to think about that.

She didn't look convinced. "I don't know, Peter. It's not like I'm going to be fishing every day."

"Think about it," he urged. He moved past her, his knees brushing hers as he headed toward the stern. "Are you hungry?"

She grinned. "I'm always hungry. One of the hazards of being a cook, I guess. Everything smells good and there's never enough time to sit down and eat."

"I've come into your life just in time," he declared, swinging the cooler in front of her and dropping it at her feet. He looked around the bay and, satisfied that they weren't in the path of any larger boats, sat down opposite Jane. "You need someone to take care of you."

Jane started to protest, but Peter opened the lid and the words died in her throat. An array of exquisite pastries sat in the top section of the cooler. "How did you get these?"

"A trip to Sandpoint took care of everything," he explained, lifting the plastic tray and setting it carefully on the deck. "There are sandwiches in here somewhere," he said, turning back to the cooler. "Turkey with hot-pepper jelly and spinach leaves." Peter looked up at her. "Sound good?"

"Sounds wonderful. You're very experienced at this," she said, noting the neat way the cans of soda pop were arranged on the ice and the plastic containers tucked in the corners.

"Not me," he admitted. "Don's wife, Linda, packed this, along with silverware borrowed from the resort." He eyed the assortment of food. "Do you think I brought too much?"

"Never," she said, pointing to a large flat carton. "What's in there?"

"German potato salad, from the deli on the Cedar Street bridge."

She eyed the container with reverence. "I've tried to make it, but never really mastered it. It's a lot of work for a side dish."

He lifted the cover and handed it to her. "Help yourself."

"Did you bring plates?"

"In that bag." He pointed to a bag behind her chair. "I'll get them." He reached over and hooked the bag with his foot and dragged it closer. "I should have designed a table for this boat."

Jane chuckled. "I don't know where you'd put it."

"Help," he groaned, trying to juggle the sandwiches and a bottle of wine on his lap.

Jane reached over and took the sandwiches from him. "If we sit on the deck, that will help."

"Good idea." He kept hold of the wine bottle and stood, finding the seat cushions that doubled as life preservers and tossing them down. Jane moved over and curled up on the deck, leaning back against the side of the boat. She took the plates out of the bag, found silverware and napkins, and arranged them neatly before her.

"Much better," she declared, as he joined her. She watched him extract the cork from the wine, rummage through the bag for wineglasses, and pour white wine into each glass. He'd gone to a lot of trouble for this, she realized, but what was he up to? Men around here didn't organize seductive sunset rides on the bay.

Or maybe they did. Maybe they did it for other women.

"What's the matter?" He handed her the glass.

"Nothing." He frowned, making lines around his beautiful mouth. Jane gulped. She remembered the feel of those lips against her skin.

"Do you want to go in to shore?"

"No. I'm fine," she assured him, and realized she meant it. The slight rocking of the boat was surprisingly soothing, and the air was exactly the perfect temperature. She glanced over her shoulder toward the western range of mountains. "I haven't been out here at sunset for years. My father and I used to do a little fishing some nights."

"Tell me about your parents," he said, unwrapping his sandwich. Simple curiosity, he told himself. The kind of question a man would ask a woman he was interested in. Perfectly innocent. Polite, even. "Have you lived here all of your life?"

"Yes. My parents grew up here, in Hope. My mother died three years ago, and my father retired shortly after that."

"Where does he live now?"

"Here, sometimes. But he finds it hard without my mother, so he travels a lot. If there's a tour advertised in the paper, he signs up and off he goes."

"And leaves you to run things."

"I don't mind. Tim manages the marina, and I take care of the restaurant. It's crazy during fishing season, but the winters are quiet."

"Any brothers or sisters?"

"No. What about you?"

"I'm an only child, too. My mother died when I was very young. My father died last year, but I have a stepmother who keeps me busy. We run the boat business together."

She smiled, amusement lighting her eyes. "So we have that in common. Only children who run boat businesses with their parents."

"And we dance well together, too." He returned her smile, holding her gaze. "We were meant to be together."

She shook her head. "You're such a flirt."

His smile faded. "You don't believe me?"

"No. Men just don't drop into town and start telling me things like, 'We were meant to be together.'"

"But I can prove it," he insisted. "Give me your glass." She did, wondering what he would do next. He was certainly the most unpredictable man she'd ever met. He placed the glass neatly beside him so that both hands were free, and leaned toward her, as if to take her face in his hands. "Ready?"

She leaned forward, unable to resist the touch of his fingers on her skin. "Ready for what?"

"This." He came closer and pressed his lips to hers. This time Jane couldn't blame her response on the champagne. She felt the warmth down to her toes, while other sensitive parts of her body reacted with alarming heat. She couldn't possibly not kiss him back, and he took advantage of her response to urge her lips apart.

The boat swayed, rocked by the wake of a passing boat, but Jane barely noticed. She wrapped her arms around Peter's neck, while his hands dropped to her neck, carefully holding her mouth against his as if he couldn't let her go, not even an inch. The kiss continued, as the sun rapidly sank toward the highest mountain peak. A slight breeze came from the mountains beyond Hope, caressing the embracing couple with cooling air, but neither felt the change in temperature. Jane only knew that kissing Peter had swept her once again into a mindless, whirling spiral of contentment.

When she finally shivered and he slowly eased away from her, his dark-eyed gaze examined her. "That proves it, you see?"

She didn't know what the hell he was talking about. Her lips were bruised, and her body ached for more. "What?" she managed, smoothing her T-shirt.

"We were meant for each other," he repeated, with great patience. "Your body knows it, whether you accept it or not."

"Lust," she declared, wishing her fogged brain would clear. She took a deep breath of the cool mountain air and exhaled slowly. She pointed to the setting sun, framed in riotous colors of rose and peach and streaked with gold. "And a romantic sunset. That's all it is."

He shook his head. "Yesterday you blamed the champagne. Tonight you blame the sunset. We could kiss each other in a basement or in the middle of the grocery store or on a mountaintop, and the effect would be the same."

Jane looked away and picked up her forgotten sandwich. There was no way on earth she would admit that Peter might just be right.

4

"ARE YOU GOING TO THE beach with me this afternoon?"

Jane flipped the line of hamburgers and reached for the buns. "I wish I could, Den, but I have to work."

"You never work after one o'clock on Mondays."

"I have to go to town today. We're almost out of meat, and I have to get groceries." She opened the buns, lined them up on the counter and flipped the hamburger patties on top of the bottom pieces.

"Your friend didn't come in for breakfast this morning."

"What friend?"

"The handsome one, the one that gave you the boat." Denise helped top the burgers with lettuce and tomato, then put them on plates. "Three of these have fries with them, two have chips."

Jane lifted the fry basket and gave it a shake before tossing the French fries onto the plates. "I didn't notice," she lied. She'd tried not to turn around every time the door opened. Don Stone hadn't been in for his usual breakfast, either, and she'd resisted asking anyone if the *Rainbow* had been seen leaving the bay. Maybe they'd gone fishing, but it was more likely that Peter had had his fun, and was on his way back to Boise with a story to tell about a short-order cook who'd fallen into his arms at every opportunity.

She was so embarrassed.

Denise took the orders and squeezed past Jane to deliver them, leaving Jane with a few minutes of free time. The lunch rush was over, and she could start cleaning up. There would be the usual afternoon coffee-and-pie customers, but few would want anything more substantial to eat. She eyed the pile of dirty dishes and decided to ignore them. Callie, the teenager who helped out with lunch, could take care of them as soon as she was finished fixing Tim another glass of Mountain Dew soda.

Ten minutes later Jane sat in a quiet booth in the far corner of the restaurant, with a plate filled with French fries and a well-cooked hamburger in front of her. Her feet hurt, but that was nothing new. She'd go down to the dock later and soak them in the lake while Tim gave her the list of supplies he'd need from town.

"Mind if I join you?"

The voice could belong only to Peter Johnson, the man she'd almost made love with two nights in a row. Jane eyed her greasy apron and winced. Why couldn't she look gorgeous and clean, for once? "No, of course not."

He slid into the seat across from her and smiled. She wished he wouldn't smile. She didn't think she could resist his sensual charm, at least not on an empty stomach. She picked up a French fry and popped it into her mouth.

"Taking a break?"

She nodded, chewed and swallowed. The damn French fry burned all the way down her throat. "Did you come for lunch? Denise will fix you something."

"I ate with Don. We went fishing this morning."

"Catch anything?"

"No, but we had a good time anyway. We went over to Garfield Bay and ate huckleberry pie."

She picked up her hamburger. "I thought you'd be on your way back to Boise by now."

He looked surprised. "Not yet."

"How long are you planning to stay in Hope?"

Peter leaned back and took his time answering. "I don't know yet. I'm supposed to be on vacation, which is fine with me. I'm not in any hurry to return to work."

"I guess if you're in charge of the company you can do anything you want to." Still, she didn't know whether to believe him or not. He didn't act like a man with a lot of responsibilities.

"Go ahead and eat," he urged. "You don't have to talk to me. I'll get a cold drink from Denise." He slid out of the booth and waved to the older waitress.

"Hi," she called. "What can I get you?"

What can I get you? Jane winced, and bit into her hamburger. No doubt he was used to women asking him that. She'd been close to asking him that herself last night. Sprawled against him in the bottom of a boat, sharing passionate kisses when they should have been sharing dinner. She'd done everything but take off her clothes and ask, *What can I get you?* She heard him chat with Denise, something about the weather and then her children, which was always good for more than a few minutes of conversation, since she had three of them. Nice kids, too; the kind of kids who respected their mother and stayed out of trouble.

She didn't know how Denise managed them all, but she envied her the big family. She'd always wanted to have a lot of children; maybe every "only child" did.

But Sean had wanted to wait, and now she couldn't help but regret that she'd gone along with his wishes. Raising a child alone would be difficult, but better than not having children at all.

She finished her lunch, drained her glass of iced tea, and wiped her mouth with a paper napkin. She leaned back in the booth and closed her eyes. She heard Peter approach the booth, hesitate, then slide in across from her again, but she didn't open her eyes. She'd tossed and turned all night; for the first time in years her bed had been too wide and too lonely.

And five-thirty had arrived painfully early.

"Are you okay?" His voice was low, concern edging his simple question.

Jane opened her eyes. She wished he wasn't quite so handsome. Sean had been big and blond, with faded blue eyes and a deceiving smile. "I'm fine."

"Denise said you're going to town."

Okay, she'd admit to herself that she was glad to see him. Jim Patrick walked by on his way to the rest room and shot them a curious look, but Jane ignored him. "I'm making the hamburger run today. I have it specially ground in Sandpoint."

"I have a couple of errands there myself. Do you want to go together?"

"But I have to go to the bank, and then I have to get groceries." There was no way he'd still want to go if it involved grocery shopping.

"So do I," Peter said. "I need to stock the cabin with a few basics, like coffee and bread. Maybe a couple of steaks. There's a barbecue grill on the front porch."

"Are you serious?"

"Yeah. It's not very big, but if I get some charcoal I—"

"No, I mean about going to town together."

"Sure." He looked surprised. "I asked you, didn't I?"

PETER CONGRATULATED himself once again. Three days in a row he'd managed to spend time with Jane Plainfield, the very *un*-plain owner of the café. He leaned against the car and waited for her to come out of the bank. He'd even found a shady place to park.

He'd tried to put Ruth's infamous list out of his mind, but it hadn't been easy. The detective was supposed to be tracking down the addresses and phone numbers of the people on that list, but Peter hadn't heard from him yet. And he'd left enough messages.

And if the long-lost niece *was* Jane Plainfield, well, he'd just have to tell her she had a relative who really wanted to meet her. But Jane didn't seem like the kind of woman who enjoyed surprises. He'd have to tell the detective not to question her. At least not until there was no alternative.

He hoped like hell she wasn't the person that his stepmother was looking for: Mitchell Parkins's illegitimate child. Jane wouldn't appreciate the news. Or the bearer of it.

Peter straightened as Jane stepped out of the bank into the sunshine. For now, his only problem would be how to convince Jane to have dinner with him. The rest could wait.

She smiled as she approached the car. "Did you get your errands done?"

"Almost. What about you?"

"The money's in the bank and the hamburger is in the coolers, so I'm happy. Now, all that's left is the grocery shopping." She moved around to the other side of the car and started to open the door.

"What about dinner?"

She stopped and gave him an odd look. "Dinner?"

"Yes. You know. Food eaten after five, with a knife and fork. You and me at a table somewhere."

She shook her head. "I can't. I make pizza tonight."

"You cook all day, every day?"

Jane ducked and entered the car. Peter slid behind the wheel and stared at her. "How many hours a day do you work?"

"It looks worse than it is. I usually take afternoons off. Wednesday is Steak Night and Friday is Seafood Night."

"And Monday is Pizza Night."

"Mondays, Tuesdays and Thursdays."

"What about Saturday and Sunday?"

"I close at five." She rummaged in her purse and pulled out a list as he backed out of the parking space and headed down the street.

"So you do have a life."

"Of course I do." She refolded her list and tucked a strand of curling hair behind her ear. "This is the busiest time of year. By the middle of November I'm sitting around counting hamburger buns."

He didn't believe her. Jane Plainfield wasn't a woman who would be content to sit around and do nothing but take inventory, but he didn't want to argue with her. He wanted to have dinner with her. He wondered if he could talk her into taking a moonlight ride on the bay. "What grocery store do you want to go to?"

Jane gave him directions, which involved heading out of town. She settled back in the leather seat of the Jeep Wagoneer. It had to be the fanciest Jeep she'd ever seen. Unlike the many others in the county, this one had yet to be abused by the harsh north Idaho winters. And every gadget invented in Detroit was on the dashboard. Baysider Boats must do pretty well, she decided—whether or not the boss was around to take care of things.

"Have you given any more thought to what you're going to do with the boat?"

She'd been expecting that question since she'd met him at the Rainbow Resort's parking area. Instead, he'd talked about winter skiing and she'd told stories about the local fishermen. "I should put a For Sale sign on it and see what happens. I still think it doesn't seem like a nice thing to do after winning it, though. Like selling a gift."

"I can always buy it back, but you'd just get the wholesale price for it. You'd probably do better selling it yourself."

"I'll talk to my father about it," she said. "He might have some ideas."

"Do you talk to him often?"

"We keep in touch." She smiled. "I'd rather have him home, but I don't tell him that." She pointed out the entrance to the supermarket. "You're sure you want to do this? It could take a while."

"I don't mind. I'll meet you back at the car."

An hour later, as she pushed her heavy cart toward the car, she saw Peter sitting behind the wheel reading the newspaper. He lifted his head as she approached and got out.

"Here," he said, opening the tailgate. "Let me get that."

"That's okay, I do this all the time."

He ignored her, instead lifting the case of lettuce out of her way and setting it in the back of the wagon. "Stand back," he said, easily transferring the other boxes of groceries from the cart to the Jeep. "There."

"Thanks. I'll be right back." Jane pushed the cart back to the front of the store and returned to the car. Peter had turned the engine on and waited for her to slide in and buckle her seat belt before he backed out of the parking spot. She could get used to this. She didn't want to get used to this. Next week it would be just her and the supplies, with no handsome, willing and sexy man loading the car and driving her home.

Jane glanced sideways at Peter, wondering if he was going to turn into a total maniac at any moment. He was simply too good to be true.

He caught her glance. "Something wrong?"

"You like women, don't you?"

Peter looked startled. "What?"

"You like women," she repeated. "You're very comfortable around them. If I didn't know you were an only child, I'd figure you grew up with three or four sisters."

"Is that a crime?"

"Is what?"

"Liking women?"

"No, of course not. I just—" She stopped. She didn't know why she'd asked him such a leading question. Did she expect him to say something like, "Oh, yes, I've made love to hundreds of women, and plan to love hundreds more," like Willie Nelson singing, "To All the Girls I've Loved Before . . ."

She'd never liked that song.

"Just what?" he urged.

"Nothing."

They rode in silence for long moments, past the wide plains that swept toward Canada, where the peaks of the Seven Sisters rose from the flatland; then into the shadows, down to the Pack River bridge. Jane automatically turned to peer into the shady slough on the right side of the road.

Peter slowed down the Jeep. "What are you looking at?"

"Sometimes the moose is in there."

"No kidding?"

"In the spring she has a baby with her." Jane searched as carefully as she could but didn't see any sign of the large animal wading at the edge of the black water. "But I don't see any sign of her today. She's usually there at dusk, or early in the morning."

"I'll have to remember to look."

She turned back to him. "Haven't you ever seen a moose before?"

"Yes, but not as close as this." They came out of the shadow of the mountain and crossed the bridge in bright sunlight, the lake shining bright and blue before them. "You should give me more credit," he said finally.

"What do you mean?"

"I told you last night that we could kiss each other in the middle of a grocery store and it would be the same as on a boat at sunset."

"What does that have to do with giving you credit?"

"In the grocery store," he explained. "I didn't try to prove it."

"Well, I would hope not!" She couldn't imagine kissing in the middle of the supermarket. She would have decked him if he'd tried.

He grinned, and she realized he was teasing her again.

"I figure you owe me." Peter shot her another teasing look before turning his attention to negotiating the curves in the road as it wound around the shore of the lake. "Dinner will do just fine."

"I have to work." Why did she regret having to say that? She had to get a grip on herself.

"I can still sit at the counter and eat a pizza, can't I?"

She couldn't be rude and disagree. "Sure. It's the least I can do."

Jane sat back in her seat and gazed at the lake. How had she been outmaneuvered so quickly?

"OH, I JUST REMEMBERED. Misty can't make it tonight." Callie looked up from refilling the coffeepot to make the announcement. Jane groaned. The groceries were put away, Peter was on his way back to the Rainbow Resort and she'd looked forward to about thirty minutes to get ready for the incoming pizza orders. She never knew if there would be two orders or twenty; there was no way to judge the food business.

And now Misty, her night waitress, wasn't showing up for work. "What did she say?"

"Timmy's sick and she can't find a sitter."

Jane looked at the clock above the bulletin board. Four-thirty. "Can you stay tonight?"

"I can't, P.J. My mom's picking me up at five and we're going to Spokane overnight for the Clint Black concert."

"That sounds like fun." It also sounded like she was working alone tonight. Jane motioned the teenager over to the counter. "How about slicing pepperoni until your mother comes?"

Callie approached the counter in what looked like slow motion and Jane suppressed the urge to sigh. It was going to be a long evening.

IT WAS GOING TO BE a long evening, Peter decided, watching Jane sprinkle cheese over sauce-covered pizza crusts. How long could one woman cook pizzas? And how many people in town were going to order them?

"No waitresses tonight?"

"No. Misty's son is sick."

A heavyset man in coveralls approached the counter. "Give me another diet cola, P.J."

"Sure." She turned around, took his cup and held it under one of the spigots.

The young man beside Peter raised his cup. "And a refill on the coffee when you have a minute?"

"No problem," she said, taking the cup as she set the soda on the counter. The bell tinkled as another customer walked in. A tourist, Peter assumed, because no one greeted the man by name when he entered.

He stepped up to the counter. "The motel down the street said I could get a pizza here," he said, frowning. "How long is it going to take?"

"About twenty minutes," Jane replied, looking at the clock on the wall as she answered.

"That long?" He made an unpleasant face, which made Peter long to take him by the collar and toss him out into the parking lot. "What's the holdup? You couldn't be that busy," he sneered. "This isn't exactly Pizza Hut."

Peter looked up at him and glared, but the man grinned as if he'd said something clever.

"No," Jane agreed, although her voice sounded tired. "This isn't Pizza Hut. What kind of pizza do you want to order?"

"A couple of large pepperoni-and-mushroom pizzas. Thick crust."

"We only have one kind of crust—not too thick and not too thin."

"Figures." He sighed. "Whatever. Guess I don't have much choice in this dump."

"Yes, you do," Peter said, standing up to look the man in the eye. "You have two," he explained, keeping his voice low. "You can go somewhere else for your dinner, or stay here and shut up."

The man's eyes widened, and he turned back to Jane. "You want me to pay for them now?"

"If you like." She wrote up the order and handed him the slip. He edged away from Peter, who watched carefully as the man counted out bills from his wallet, then retreated to a seat in a corner booth.

The young man beside him gave Peter a thumbs-up sign as he slid back onto the stool. "Nice goin'," he whispered.

"Thanks." He waited for Jane to say something, but the buzzer went off in the back room and she disappeared to retrieve a pizza from the oven. He'd expected to flirt and talk with Jane, keep her amused with his witty banter while she assembled pizzas on the other side of the counter. But that plan hadn't worked. She'd been cooking since he arrived, and even by ordering a pepperoni pizza he hadn't distracted her from her work.

"Here's your pizza," she said, dumping a small flat box in front of him.

Peter looked back at her. "No plate?"

"No charge. And you're not eating it here." Her hazel eyes flashed at him, and her cheeks were flushed from the heat. "You're on your way home."

"No, I'm eating it here." He wished he could unwrap the apron from around her body and fit his hands around her waist. And higher.

"Not unless you keep quiet and let me run my business myself."

"That guy was being a jerk."

"So? It's my business and he's my jerk to deal with."

Peter shook his head. "No one is going to treat you like that. At least not in front of me."

"And what gives you the right to act like my protector?"

He opened his mouth. The three men at the counter leaned closer to hear his answer, but Peter decided to say nothing. *Because we've almost made love twice* wouldn't be a popular reason. And he didn't want a hot pizza deposited on his head, either.

She pushed his pizza box forward, urging him to take it before it fell in his lap, and then returned to the back room as the buzzer sounded once again.

The men gave Peter sympathetic looks as he stood to leave. He knew she would be aggravated if he left a tip, so he dropped a dollar on the counter before he headed for the door, the pizza box gripped in his hand. He would eat his dinner on the porch overlooking Lake

Pend Oreille, and he would forget all about Plain Jane Plainfield and her intriguing kisses.

JANE REACHED FOR THE gallon jug of white vinegar and poured a generous puddle on the hot surface of the grill. Pungent steam rose immediately, making her wrinkle her nose. Every night she performed this ritual and it never got easier. Even the exhaust fan couldn't sweep up the odor fast enough.

She looked at the clock as she pulled on her heavy work gloves and reached for the scrubbing pad. Only nine-fifteen, and it felt like midnight. She hadn't had a good night's sleep since the barbecue. Since meeting Peter.

Jane turned back to the grill. She would not think about Peter Johnson and his laughing brown eyes. Or his very tempting mouth. Or the way his hands felt on her breasts.

Jane scrubbed. Faster. Harder. In time to the music on the Spokane radio station. She backed up for a breath of cleaner air, satisfied she'd removed the worst of the black, and heard her name. She switched off the fan and turned to see Peter Johnson standing at the front door.

"We're closed," she hollered. Why did he have to come here when she reeked of vinegar and grease? She eyed the crusty work gloves and gingerly pulled them off. He wasn't going to go away, that was obvious. She might as well let him in and find out what he wanted.

She crossed the dark dining area, unlocked the door, let him step inside and locked it behind him. "What are you doing here, Peter? I'm through for the night."

"I came to walk you home."

"I live next door," she reminded him. She gestured around the room. "And I can't leave until this place is cleaned up."

"Then I'll help you clean up."

"You'll help me clean up?" she echoed, sounding stupid even to herself. "Why?"

He shrugged. "Thought since you were short a waitress, you might need a hand," he explained, waving toward the dirty tables. "And it looks like I'm right."

"You don't have to do this."

"Of course, I don't," he agreed, the familiar light in his eyes making her heart pound faster. "But it's an excuse to see you again."

Jane shook her head. "We were together all afternoon."

"But not alone," he countered. "You have an extra sponge?"

Jane backed up, trying to regain her composure. "Sure. Follow me to the sink. You can clear the rest of the tables and wipe down the counters."

"No problem," he said, close behind her.

She pointed to the sink. "Watch out. The water gets very hot." Then she pulled on the gloves and grabbed a roll of paper towels. "I'm going to finish the grill."

He paused to watch her wipe black goo from the dull surface of the grill. "You have to do this every night?"

"Yes," she said, refolding the wad of paper towel. "Unless you want your omelet to taste like hamburgers tomorrow morning." She watched as he found the dishcloth and gingerly lifted it from the soapy water. He gave it a careful squeeze, then turned to wipe the counter.

"Do you want this coffee machine on?"

"No," she said, continuing to wipe the grill. This was the second step, with two more to go. "There's a switch on the front."

"Got it," he said. "Any special place for dirty dishes?"

"Either in the sink or on the ledge behind the counter. I'll get to them when I finish this."

"All right." He began to whistle along with the radio. Jane returned to cleaning the grill and tried to pretend that he was really a male version of Misty, not a sexy stranger with a wicked smile. If she couldn't concentrate on her work, well, she could blame it on the smell of vinegar.

When the grill was polished, smoothed and gleaming, Jane turned her attention to washing dishes. Mostly silverware and coffee cups, the stack was high, since she hadn't had a waitress to help her keep up with the dirty dishes during the evening.

Her feet throbbed, but the thick black mat cushioned her soles as much as possible. It was one of the things she'd invested in when the Schoonovers failed to renew the lease and moved to Montana two years ago. She'd agreed to take over the café, at least until her father had found someone else to lease it. Two years later and she was still cleaning the grill every night.

"I'm finished," Peter declared, coming up next to her. "Should I dry those?"

"No. Denise will put them away in the morning."

"Are you finished?"

"Just about." She unplugged the sink and let the water run down the drain. Peter handed her a dish towel, but before she could completely dry her hands he tugged one of them, pulling her from behind the counter into the center of the dining room.

"They're playing our song," he informed her, sweeping her into his arms.

"'All My Exes Live in Texas'? How romantic."

"That's okay," he said, holding her tightly as he began the two-step. "It's a good excuse to dance, don't you think?"

"This is crazy." She looked over his shoulder as headlights flashed by on the highway. "What if someone sees us?"

He spun her around. "You sure worry about what people think, don't you?"

"I don't like thinking people are talking about me."

"No one's going to know you actually took a few minutes to enjoy yourself," Peter assured her.

Jane wished she could agree with him. She wanted to lean against him and let him lead her around the room, but dancing in her apron felt strange; and dancing in the middle of the café even stranger. When the song ended, Clint Black began his latest version of "Desperado," a slower song than the previous one.

She wished she wasn't such a sucker for country ballads. And handsome strangers. Seemed like the combination had gotten her into this mess in the first place.

Some women wouldn't call this a "mess."

"Why the sigh?" Peter asked, looking down at her.

"I guess it just slipped out." His eyes were the color of maple syrup.

He smiled. "Is my dancing that bad?"

"You know it isn't." Jane sighed again. "That's the trouble. Why are you doing this?"

Peter stopped dancing, but didn't take his hand from around Jane's waist or drop her hand. "I like you."

She had to give him credit for not acting like he didn't understand her question. "But—"

"And I like being with you," he added, his mouth nearing hers. "I don't know why you want to argue about it. I've liked you since the first time I saw you, and I thought the feeling was mutual."

He kissed her then—not a tentative kiss, but one full of promise and passion. Jane's fingers tightened on his shoulder, holding him as their lips met in an achingly familiar embrace. She'd been kissing him for three days; she felt as if she'd been kissing him forever.

When they finally parted, when he lifted his mouth from hers, he murmured, "First time on land."

She had to think for a minute, then heat flushed her cheeks. "It didn't seem to make any difference."

"No," he agreed. "None at all." He dropped his hands to her waist and looked down at her. "Now what?"

"The song's over, and the café is cleaned up, so we say good-night."

He didn't look too pleased with her reply, but he dropped his hands and backed up a step. "All right. I'll wait for you to lock up."

"I have to put the money away."

"I'll wait."

Still shaky from the kiss, Jane turned to the cash register and punched the button that allowed the cash drawer to pop open. She took a red pouch from underneath the shelf and tossed all the bills inside, then zipped it shut. She'd count the money later, when her heart stopped pounding at sixty miles an hour.

"I'll walk you home," Peter said, standing by the door as if he were guarding her from a pack of escaped convicts.

"You really don't—" But she saw the stubborn expression on his face and realized she was wasting her breath. For some reason this man thought she needed protecting, so she may as well accept it.

Besides, it was kind of nice to have someone think of her as a woman—not as a cook, buddy or fish-photographer. Sometimes she felt like everybody's daughter, and there was nothing wrong with that, but she secretly preferred the way Peter Johnson's eyes lit up when he looked at her, and the sexy slash of his lips when she said something that annoyed him and he didn't know whether to laugh or frown.

He was a dangerous man, she realized, turning off the lights above the kitchen area. She could fall in love with a man like this.

And she'd fall flat on her face in the process.

5

"WHAT DO YOU MEAN, you hadn't thought of it?" Roger looked incredulous, then thanked her as she refilled his coffee cup. Jane poured herself a cup of coffee and leaned on the counter. The mayor would certainly have more to say, so she might as well make herself comfortable now that the breakfast orders were filled.

"Well, I didn't," she said, refusing to feel guilty about not entering the boat regatta. She took a sip of coffee and waited for his protests.

"You have to. Everyone's going to want to see the Bodacious Barbecue prize, you know. It's good advertising for next year's ticket sales."

"I'll let you borrow the boat, Roger. You can decorate it and drive it around the bay all weekend, if you like."

"I have my own boat, P.J. You know that. And the grandchildren are counting on being in it with me Sunday morning."

"Whose idea was this, anyway? We've never had a boat parade before."

"*Regatta*," he corrected. "The chamber of commerce thought it up. Coeur d'Alene's had some success with it. We're going to decorate the boats and parade around in the bay. Don Stone's going to be the judge. He's got the biggest boat at this end of the bay, anyway, so he's going to lead us around once, then watch us go by a second time."

"Just in the bay?"

He nodded. "Yeah. It'll be nice and calm first thing in the morning, honey. You shouldn't have any qualms at all."

"Your boyfriend just drove up," Tim announced, nodding toward the parking lot.

Roger frowned. "Whose boyfriend?"

"P.J.'s."

"I don't have a boyfriend, Tim." She glared at him.

"Well, you were dancing with someone last night when the restaurant was closed."

"Does everyone in town have to know my personal business?" She quickly refastened her ponytail and hoped she didn't look too disheveled.

Roger turned to see Peter enter the café. "Hasn't he gone back to Boise yet?"

"Obviously not," Jane murmured, hoping she sounded casual. Of course, someone would have seen them dancing last night. Jane turned back to her mechanic. "Don't you have gas to pump or an engine to fix?"

"I'm waiting for a customer," he said, winking at her. "No need to get cranky, P.J."

"I'm not—"

"Good morning," Peter drawled, approaching the counter. He slid onto the empty stool beside Roger as if they'd been saving it for him. And maybe they had, Jane mused, noting Tim's smirk.

"Hi."

Denise hurried over. "Hi, Peter. The usual? Mexican omelet, with hash browns and white toast?"

"How'd you remember that?"

"It's my job," she said, pleased. "I'll get you a cup of coffee."

"Thanks." He looked over at Tim and Roger. "Good morning. Am I interrupting anything?"

Roger shook his head. "No. I'm just trying to talk P.J. into entering the boat regatta."

"When is that?"

Jane answered for him. "This weekend. Sunday morning, to be exact." Then she picked up her coffee cup and moved it over to the counter beside the grill. She started fixing his omelet, but she listened carefully to the conversation behind her. Just in case anyone asked her a question, of course.

Denise seemed content to take Jane's place at the counter. "My kids are sure looking forward to seeing it."

"Have you entered?"

"We don't have a boat."

"You can take the Baysider," Peter said. "Right, Jane?"

"I don't know how to run a boat," Denise protested. "And I don't want to learn with three children on board."

"Jane and I will take you," Peter offered. "Won't we, Jane?"

We? "But aren't you going to be on Don's boat?"

"I could, I suppose, but I'd rather help you out."

Roger grinned. "Well, that certainly solves everyone's problems. It's an international theme, Peter," he explained. "You just decorate your boat like a country. And there's a ten-dollar entry fee, to cover the cost of the prizes."

"Prizes?" Denise echoed. "This is sounding better and better."

"First prize is a microwave, second prize is a food processor, and third prize is a gift certificate somewhere. I can't remember where."

Peter looked at Jane and winked. She turned back to the grill and poured his eggs onto the hot surface.

"Here's our entry fee," she heard him tell Roger.

"Well, I just happen to have some forms here in my pocket," the mayor drawled. "You fill this out while you're waiting for your breakfast, and then you're official. I just knew I could get that boat in the parade!"

"Don't gloat, Roger," Jane warned, turning to collect the chopped vegetables for Peter's omelet.

"Well, I'm happy," he grumbled. "We needed at least ten entries and now we've got 'em."

"Pretty good odds for winning a prize, I'd say. Could you pass the sugar down here?"

"Sure, son. You done any fishing this week?"

"Just one day, out on the *Rainbow*, but we didn't catch anything. Didn't even get a bite."

"Come back in November, for the derby. The big ones come to the surface then."

"I'll remember that," Peter said.

Jane arranged slices of bread in the toaster and flipped Peter's omelet over on its side. She put a lid on top of it so the cheese would melt, then turned to the men facing her across the counter. Denise was over in the corner taking another order.

She met Peter's laughing gaze. "What country are you going to be?"

Peter shrugged. "I don't care. You pick."

"No way. I don't remember agreeing to this."

"Sure, you did," he replied, undaunted by her protest. "You volunteered the Baysider."

"No, *you* volunteered the Baysider. I have to work."

His expression fell. "Take the morning off."

"Sunday mornings are one of the busiest times," she told him. "I can't leave." Peter Johnson was a man who got his own way too often for his own good—at least as far as she was concerned.

Denise came up in time to hear their conversation. "We're going to have a lot of fun. You don't have to work this Sunday and you know it, so quit teasing." She turned to Peter and refilled his coffee cup. "She'll be there. I guarantee it. So, how about Africa? I can make some animals out of cardboard and the kids can paint them."

"Africa?" Jane shook her head. "That's a continent. You have to pick a country, like Kenya."

"All right," Denise agreed, winking at Peter so Jane could see her. "Kenya it is. Any objections?"

"No," he said.

"No," Jane said, deciding she'd better help them out. "I'll get some animal-skin fabric for our costumes."

Peter choked. "Costumes?"

"Of course." Jane picked up the pitcher of pancake batter and poured neat circles on the grill top. "If I'm going to take the morning off, I want us to give it our best shot."

Denise nodded. "You're on a lucky streak, that's for sure."

"I never thought of it like that." Jane eyed the rest of the order Denise clipped to the hood above the grill. Nothing fancy, just hotcakes and bacon. She took her spatula and moved several slices of half-cooked bacon to the front where it would fry quickly.

"You should," Denise told her. "You haven't had this much excitement in your life since Sean—"

"Never mind," Jane interrupted, hoping to keep Denise from repeating stories about her ex-husband. He'd become something of a legend in Hope, and a story about him could surface every time someone wanted to exchange "I knew a guy who was so stupid . . ." stories.

"Who's Sean?"

Peter certainly didn't miss anything, which might explain why he was president of his own company. She turned to flip the hotcakes. "My ex-husband."

"Where is he now?"

"California, last I heard."

"Well, that's far away enough." Peter sounded pleased.

"Africa would be even better," she muttered, flipping the bacon over. Then she fixed Peter's plate and set it in front of him.

"Thanks." He smiled, and Jane's stomach flipped over. "I can see why this becomes a habit around here."

Roger picked up his coffee cup. "This is our second home," he agreed.

"Did you grow up in Hope?" Peter asked, reaching for the salt and pepper. Jane turned back to the hotcakes, but she listened to his conversation with the mayor.

"Yep, with Jane's dad. Boy, we sure had some good times together." He raised his voice. "When's that father of yours coming back where he belongs?"

Jane shrugged. "He'll show up one of these days," she said, hoping she didn't sound too homesick for him. "He took the camper and headed to Vancouver about six weeks ago. Last time he called, he'd gone up into Alaska to visit some old friends."

Peter kept the conversation going. "Mr. Plainfield grew up here, too?"

"Sure did. There were a bunch of us hell-raisers in those days. We did a lot to keep food on the table then, back when we were young. But we still found time to do some fishin'."

"Yes," Jane agreed, filling plates with hotcakes. "My mother knew how to cook fish fifty different ways."

"Who else grew up here?"

"Well, let's see," Roger drawled, taking a sip of his coffee. "There were six of us, I guess. Chet Plainfield and Jim Patrick married early, but we still had some wild times. Danny Butler lives over in Clark Fork, Miles Ruen is still on Spring Creek Hill, and Mitch Parkins died years ago."

Jane turned to listen, sure she would hear a story she hadn't heard before.

"How?"

"Oh—" the older man frowned "—boating accident. Freak storm came up."

"Dad doesn't talk about it," Jane mused. "I think Mitch Parkins was one of his closest friends."

Peter shot her a curious look, then turned back to Roger. "Does he still have family around here?"

"There might be a cousin somewhere." He shrugged. "Rest moved away years ago."

Jane watched disappointment cross Peter's face. "Why are you so interested?"

"I like history," he explained. "Especially in small towns. I, uh, knew someone who came up here in 1963, and I just wondered what the town was like thirty years ago."

Roger shook his head. "1963. The year Parkins drowned." He stood to leave, tossing three dollars on the counter. "You can wonder all you like, son. But sometimes it's best to leave it alone."

PETER WISHED HE COULD take the mayor's advice, but Ruth Parkins Johnson would not be so easily convinced. And she'd be calling again to find out what progress he'd made, so he decided he'd better have something to report. He couldn't stay in Hope for the rest of the summer, no matter how tempting the thought of breakfast each morning, prepared by Jane and served by her easygoing waitress was.

So he got into the Jeep and headed to Spokane, slowing down to see if the moose stood in the pond by the Pack River bridge, and south. To find some answers.

After all, he consoled himself as he left the sight of the sparkling lake, the sooner he solved the mystery of the Parkins child, the sooner he could concentrate on Jane Plainfield. He'd never met a woman like her.

He'd never met a woman who kissed him in that searing, hungry way. And she didn't even realize it. He stepped on the gas, edging above the speed limit. The sooner he got there, the sooner he could be back in Hope. After all, tomorrow was Wednesday. Steak Night at the café.

"MAKE THE DETECTIVE do more to earn his money, or I'll replace him."

"Ruth, he's the best there is," Peter explained patiently. "That's why you hired him, but you're not his only client, and he's managed to get a lot of information. I don't want to know how." He turned to watch Don's boat coming in toward the dock. It was one of the biggest Baysiders they made, and she looked good. He waved, but Don didn't see him. Peter turned back to the papers on the kitchen table while his aunt complained.

"He gave me some leads to follow myself," he said, hoping to placate her. "Things I can do at the local courthouse in Sandpoint. And I've been asking around about Mitch, but so far no one's had much to say." He listened. "No, I haven't mentioned your name yet. Your detective told me to keep my mouth shut."

He listened to Ruth's instructions for another minute, then gently managed to steer the conversation over to Baysider. After making several decisions and promising to call his assistant and plant manager, Peter was free to hang up the phone and watch Don dock the boat. He hurried outside and crossed the rocky beach to the wharf.

"Hey!" his friend called. "Where've you been?"

"Spokane."

"Any luck?"

"Not really. We crossed off two more names." He stepped onto the dock and helped Don unload the fishing gear. "Catch anything?"

"Just a small rainbow. I threw it back." He tipped his hat back and grinned. "Is our favorite cook still on the list?"

"Unfortunately."

Don shook his head. "I don't know Chet Plainfield very well, Pete, but he's a decent man who seems to think the world of his daughter. And I've never heard that Janie was adopted. But it's not a subject that comes up very often, I'll say that."

"Want to go out to dinner?"

Don grinned. "Steak Night? Linda and I never miss it."

PETER JOHNSON IN A loincloth was something Jane had never imagined. But it was certainly a sight to behold, despite the fact that he wore it draped over a pair of simple black bathing trunks. The regatta was only one hour away, and everyone had been anxious to try on their "African" outfits. Peter declared it added to their creativity while they constructed the animals, and no one disagreed with him.

"Like it?" He held up a Styrofoam giraffe for her inspection. Denise had rounded up large chunks of Styrofoam and cardboard from her brother-in-law, the one who owned the building-supply store.

"Very nice."

He frowned. "That's all you can say? Robbie and I worked very hard on the brown spots." The little boy next to him grinned.

"It's totally awesome," Jane declared, hoping she'd found the right words to please the children. Angela, Denise's twelve-year-old daughter, smiled at her, but ten-year-old Jimmy was busy painting an enormous piece of cardboard gray.

"I got the trunk," Denise announced, dragging a length of metal hose out of her truck and spreading it in front of Jane's trailer.

"What is it?"

"It used to be the hose you connect your clothes dryer to, to vent the air outside. Now it's an elephant's trunk."

"Brilliant," Peter told her. "But how are we going to attach it to the elephant?"

"I'm done!" Jimmy put down his gray brush and stepped back. "I just need to paint on the eyes."

The rest of them studied it, nodding their approval.

"Can we tape the animals to the boat?"

"I think so," Peter said. "Or we'll tie them. It's not very windy. Let's hope it stays that way."

Jane agreed, silently praying for calm waters. She'd agreed to this mostly for her friend's sake, but she was questioning her sanity. Why had she suggested the costumes? She wore a red one-piece suit, but she still felt naked, even with the print fabric draped like a sarong around her.

"I have some masking tape in the shop," she offered. Now, if she could tape it over her mouth before she agreed to anything else that involved Peter Johnson and boating on the bay.

Denise looked at her watch. "I hope that's fast-drying paint. We're running out of time."

"We'll make it," Peter said, earning another smile from little Robbie. "No problem, huh, Rob?"

"No problem," the child repeated, edging closer to his new hero.

Jane shared a smile with Peter, then looked away. He was so gorgeous and so appealing, and she wished she could steal Ed Kennedy's tugboat for another moon-lit ride. Which just proved she should stick to cooking and forget men. This one was a heartbreaker of mega-proportions.

He lives in Boise. She promised to chant it, as a reminder of reality.

"What?" Denise looked at her.

"Nothing," Jane answered. "I'll get the tape."

"Your lips were moving."

"I was just praying for calm waters," she assured her.

Peter put his arm around her, making her want to run. Making her want to bury her face in his leopard spots. "You'll be fine. I'll take care of everything."

"Music," Angela declared. "We need music."

"What kind?"

"I have my boom box. Maybe we can find an African station."

"An African station? From Spokane?"

"Why not?"

"It seems a little farfetched to me," Jane admitted. "But go ahead and bring it."

"We want to win the second prize," Denise reminded her. "I want that food processor. I've *always* wanted a food processor."

"I heard it's a Sunbeam, too."

"I want it," Denise repeated, painting a black eye on the elephant. "And this elephant is going to get it for me."

"Positive thinking," Peter agreed, winking at Jane. "I like your style."

"Thank you," Denise replied, stepping back to examine her elephant. "What do you think?"

Jane laughed. "I hear the sound of vegetables being ground to a pulp."

Robbie tugged on her arm. "Can we go in the boat now?"

"Sure," she said. "Let's carry the animals down to the dock and see if Peter can figure out how to make sure they don't blow away."

"Robbie and I will do our best," Peter declared, lifting a giraffe. "I hope this is fast-drying paint."

"It is," she assured him, wishing he wasn't quite so muscular. He must spend a lot of time at a Boise health club. When he wasn't designing boats, that is. Jane turned away. She had to keep reminding herself that Peter Johnson was only a temporary visitor—one who would not be easily content living at the slow pace of a remote northern town.

Still, she resolved, stepping onto the dock, she could enjoy Peter's company for the remaining days of his vacation. As long as she kept it platonic, she'd have no regrets when he left for home.

"AND THE FIRST PRIZE, a brand-new Panasonic microwave oven, goes to . . . Thailand!"

Jane breathed a sigh of relief. The Fitzpatrick boat had been the obvious choice for first place. Cardboard elephants couldn't compete with belly dancers and an enormous genie. Second place would not be so clear, though.

"Cross your fingers," Denise told her kids.

Peter stood behind Jane, his hands on her shoulders, as they waited with the rest of the crowd at the Floating Restaurant for Roger to announce the rest of the regatta winners. She told herself she couldn't move away because there were so many people around them. She leaned back slightly, to test the solid feel of Peter's chest, then quickly straightened as his fingers tightened on her bare shoulders.

"Excuse me," she mumbled, hoping she wasn't blushing again. She wished she could outgrow that particular reaction, but there was something about Peter Johnson that triggered it.

"Second prize sure stumped our judges, but the Sunbeam food processor goes to..." Roger paused for dramatic effect. "The Andersons, of the U.S.A.!"

Jane applauded politely, and dared a glance at Denise, who shrugged. The Andersons, dressed in red, white and blue, accepted their prize and waved American flags.

"Too bad," Peter whispered in her ear.

"Third and final prize, an Oster blender, goes to the boat with the most ambitious design...the one with the wild animals...Plain Jane's Café!"

Jane pushed Denise forward to accept the prize. "Go ahead. It was all your idea."

Denise and the kids had their picture taken, then joined Peter and Jane by the door.

"Thanks," Denise said. "It was a great morning, and the kids really had a good time."

"Come on," Peter said. "We'll head back to the marina."

"I'll meet you there," Denise said. "John gets through here in a few minutes, then we'll all come over to help clean up the boat."

Jane shook her head. "Don't bother. You and your husband enjoy your day off. There isn't that much to do, anyway."

"And I'll help," Peter added, taking Jane's hand and tugging her toward the door.

Denise started to smile. "You two want to be alone, huh? Okay, I can take a hint. See you tomorrow!"

"We don't—" Jane began, but Peter opened the door and urged her onto the dock.

"Come on," he said. "We have a beautiful summer day, a great boat, and all the time in the world to enjoy both of them."

"*You* might have all the time in the world, but I don't." She blinked against the bright sun and wished she hadn't left her sunglasses on the boat.

"Sure, you do," he countered, handing her into the Baysider. "We're going to go back to the marina, ditch the wildlife, make some sandwiches, and spend the rest of the day on the lake."

"On the lake?"

He untied the boat from its mooring. "On the bay, then. We'll stay close to shore, although I wanted to go around to the other side of the peninsula and check out some property Don told me about."

Jane forgot to argue about his plans for her time. "You're interested in buying property around here?"

"Not me. A friend of mine is always looking for investments, and Don keeps talking about the rising value of lakefront property."

"That's true," she agreed, a little disappointed. But why should she be disappointed if he didn't buy land around here? It wasn't as if she wanted him to stick around.

He hopped on board. "Do you want to start her up this time?"

"Sure. Why not?" When he looked surprised, she added, "It's not as if I've never steered a boat before. It's just not one of my favorite things, that's all."

He held up his hands in mock surrender. "Fine. Take her out, captain."

She grinned, ducking under the canopy to the instrument panel. "I believe I will. I'm going to keep her close to shore, though."

"One question," Peter said, pretending to be serious. The glint in his eyes gave him away. "Can we take off our loincloths now?"

Jane turned away and hid her sigh. If she wasn't careful, she'd be taking off a lot more than her loincloth. As soon as they reached the marina she'd grab an oversize T-shirt, a bottle of sunscreen and her father's fishing gear. If she was going to spend the rest of the day with Peter Johnson, she should be protected. And she should have something to do.

6

"THAT WASN'T TOO BAD, was it?"

Jane lay stretched out on the beach, smooth rocks making a surprisingly comfortable mattress. She closed her eyes against the sun. "Umm."

His footsteps crunched as he came closer. Then he sat down beside her, blocking part of the afternoon sun. "You didn't scream or turn pale or ask me to take over the steering wheel."

"Uh-uh," she managed, feeling sleepy and lazy and totally decadent.

"Hey." He nudged her. "Are you going to sleep?"

She couldn't have opened her eyes without a struggle. "No."

"Liar."

Jane didn't have the energy to argue. She heard him paw through the rocks, then heard one hit the water.

"I'll just sit here and skip rocks while you sleep. If you're lucky I'll save you some lunch."

"You'd better."

A shadow crossed her eyelids as he bent over her, brushing a quick kiss on her lips. "I promise," he said, his voice a low caress.

"Don't do that," she murmured. "Someone might see."

"Like who? We're on a very small, very private beach. There's no one around, except for a few boats out on the water. We could make love right here and no one would ever know."

Her eyes flew open. "*I* would know. You can't just—" Too late she saw the laughter in his eyes.

"Yes," he agreed, dropping his gaze to her mouth. "When I make love to you, you *will* know."

"Stop your teasing," she said, even though she knew he was no longer teasing. "And let me sleep." Though how she was going to sleep with her skin tingling, she had no idea.

He rolled away from her. "All right. I'll leave you alone, but it's only temporary."

Jane closed her eyes again, and listened to the crunch of his footsteps as he walked away. She heard his shout of surprise as he dived into the cold water, and tried not to laugh. She wished he wasn't quite so much fun.

And she wished he wasn't quite so tempting.

SUNSETS WERE HIS downfall, Peter decided. Especially sunsets framed by mountains and witnessed from the middle of a tranquil bay. And shared with a beautiful woman. He leaned back and eyed the "beautiful woman" next to him.

"What?"

"Nothing," he answered. "I was just thinking that this is what vacations are all about."

She turned her attention back to the sunset. "I love this time of day."

"But you can't see the sunset from the restaurant window."

"I don't work every night."

"If you didn't close early on Sundays you'd be there now."

She sighed. "Don't remind me."

He took her hand and frowned at the red blotches that covered her fair skin. "How'd you get into this business, anyway? Cooking classes in college?"

She laughed. "No. I was a business major, determined to learn as much as I could in order to run the marina with my father. I used to feel bad that I wasn't a boy, because Dad obviously needed a son to help out."

He touched each rough fingertip with gentle movements. "I'm sure your father never regretted having you for his daughter." He waited, wondering if she would reveal that she was adopted. And what he would say if she did. He held his breath, pausing at her little finger.

"I hope not," she said after a long moment.

He kept her hand in his. "You didn't answer my question."

"About the café?"

"Yes." She hadn't noticed he was still holding her hand, so he didn't let it go.

"Dad built the café about five years ago and leased it to some people from Spokane. Dad thought the fishermen needed someplace to eat on this side of the lake. The Floating Restaurant is only open nights and weekends, and is closed during the worst months of the winter. Same with the Litehouse, on the other side of the Rainbow Resort."

"So how did you end up with it?"

"The people from Spokane just couldn't get used to small-town life and didn't renew their lease. I took it over, right after my divorce. I thought it would keep me busy, and I was right."

"Too busy," he said.

She shrugged. "Maybe. In the summer."

"The best time of year."

She looked at him and shook her head. "I like three feet of snow on the ground and a fire in the woodstove and having movies to watch on the VCR."

He chuckled. "You lead an exciting life, Jane Plainfield. Do you go completely wild and make popcorn, too?"

She didn't seem to mind his teasing, which was another thing he liked about her. "Sure. Sometimes I don't even wait for the weekend."

The sun dropped behind the highest mountain peak, leaving trails of gold in the sky to light the clouds. This time Peter was prepared for the evening breeze, and he grabbed sweatshirts from the pile of clothes at his feet. He released Jane's hand long enough to let her put on her shirt, and then urged her to sit between his legs so she could lean back against his chest and watch the fading colors in the sky in comfort.

It was a fine thing, Peter decided, to hold a warm and relaxed woman in his arms, to rest his chin on her hair and inhale the scent of apple-blossom shampoo while he watched the sky darken over the mountaintop. Lights sparkled on the hill of East Hope, and from somewhere on land a mother called for her children to come home.

What would it matter if Jane was really Ruth's niece? He tightened his arms around her waist, thinking he could hold on to her for a long, long time. After she got over the shock, she'd become part of the family. Part of another boat business, he assumed, knowing Ruth's commitment to family ties.

But he didn't like keeping secrets. He liked things out in the open, and sneaking around trying to find some long-lost relative was not something he enjoyed. And whether or not Jane was adopted was none of his business.

He would contact the detective tomorrow and urge him to hurry. He wanted to concentrate on making Jane a part of his life in a much, much different way.

Later, when they'd docked the boat for the night, he walked her back to her mobile home. He didn't wait for her to invite him in. Instead he kissed her—one passionate kiss full of promise, just to give her something to think about—and left her standing in the circle of light from the nearby streetlamp.

"HE SAYS HE DIDN'T want his eggs over easy." Denise put the plate on the counter beside the grill.

"He's had them over easy every morning for the past six months." Jane shook her head, trying not to laugh. "How does he want them?"

Denise shrugged. "He said, 'Anything but over easy.' Do you think Elroy's getting a little senile?"

"Maybe." Jane slid the eggs back onto the grill. "I'll cook them a little longer, break the yolks to make them different." She looked over her shoulder as the door swung open, but the tall man that entered wasn't Peter. Damn. She looked at the clock above the sink and sighed. After eight, which was still early if you were a Boise tourist.

"Watching for someone special?"

Jane ignored Denise's grin. "No."

"Yeah, right." She clipped another order to the line of green slips above Jane's head. "Busy morning, even though Mr. Handsome hasn't showed up. Did you have fun yesterday?"

"We went for a boat ride and a picnic." She pierced Elroy's eggs and waited a moment, then slipped them back on his plate. "There. I hope this makes him happy."

"Me, too." She grabbed the plate and grinned. "A boat ride and a picnic? Sounds romantic."

"It was," she admitted, thinking of Peter's arms around her, warming her against the chill of the evening breeze. Trouble was, she wasn't used to romance. Or good-night kisses. She'd been divorced too long to remember either one.

"Good. I like that man." Denise hurried off with the plate and a carafe of fresh coffee, and Jane turned back to the grill. French toast, hotcakes, omelets and fried eggs all waited to be cooked. With the accompanying hash browns and bacon, of course.

"Hey, P.J.," Tim called. "Saw you fishin' yesterday. How's the boat working?"

"Just fine." She braced herself for the inevitable teasing.

A deep voice boomed from the corner booth. "She was out in a boat all by herself?"

"No." Tim chuckled. "She wasn't alone."

"Who were you with, P.J.?" one of the older men asked.

Jane concentrated on pouring hotcake batter onto the grill. "A friend."

"A male friend?" someone else asked, mischief in his voice.

Jane turned around to glare at her mechanic. "See what you started? I'll never hear the end of it."

Roger slid onto the end stool and removed his cap. "Never hear the end of what? Winning third prize?" Denise slid a cup of coffee in front of him. "You did a great job with that boat. Too bad you lost one of the giraffes."

"It was windier than we thought," Jane admitted. "Denise is happy with winning the blender, though."

"I'm going to try for the food processor next year," Denise informed the six men at the counter. "Unless the tips around here get bigger."

The men laughed, and Jane concentrated on her cooking, glad that attention had been diverted from her boat trip with Peter.

"Was that your boat docked over by the point yesterday afternoon?"

She didn't turn around. "Probably. We— I was there for about an hour."

"Thought so," Cliff said, but being a man of few words he didn't say anything else, to Jane's relief. She hoped that Peter would come in and say hello, and yet she hoped he would stay away, although his arrival for breakfast every morning was now being taken for granted by the rest of the regular customers. They didn't seem surprised when he sat at the counter right behind the grill and talked to her while she cooked his omelet. She looked at the clock again. He was usually here by now.

"You have plans for the day?" Roger asked.

"Nothing special. Why?"

"You keep looking at the clock."

"I can't believe it's still morning," she fibbed. *I can't believe I'm watching the door, waiting for Peter Johnson to walk in.* She turned back to her cooking, determined to concentrate on feeding her customers, but the morning continued to drag. It was eleven o'clock before she finally admitted to herself that Peter wasn't coming in for breakfast. Don Stone hadn't come in, either, so they were probably out fishing. Jane switched on the deep-fat fryer, took the ground sirloin from the refrigerator and began preparing for the noon rush.

She gave the door one more hopeful glance before turning back to the mound of beef on the counter. Maybe he'd come in for lunch instead.

He didn't. By the time she left the café to Denise and headed for town, Jane decided she'd better get a grip on herself. A few boat rides and a few kisses and she was acting like a lovesick teenager. Not at all becoming for a woman of thirty, that was for certain. She had more important things to think about, anyway, like making the bank deposit and placing an ad for Seafood Night in the paper.

"How much is the two-inch space?" Jane examined the samples the clerk at the *Daily Bee* had given her and debated whether or not to spend the extra money. She had to fry a lot of fish to pay for an ad, but it could be worth it. She finally decided on the size and began to write a check for the amount when she heard a familiar voice.

"Thanks for your help," she heard Peter say. She looked up to see him step out of a back room with an older man behind him.

"I hope you got everything you need. The library is another source, but I'm not sure if they go back to 1963." The two men shook hands, and Peter turned to leave.

He hesitated when his gaze met Jane's, but he recovered quickly and managed a casual smile. "Well, hello. What are you doing here?"

She noticed he tucked the sheaf of papers under his arm so the print wasn't visible. It looked like a stack of photocopies. "Placing an ad for Seafood Night, trying to drum up some new customers."

"You don't have enough?"

"Not on Friday nights. We compete with the fancier restaurants then." She glanced at the papers and back to his face. He definitely looked uncomfortable. "What are you up to this afternoon?"

"Research," he said quickly. "Historical research."

"Oh?"

He didn't explain, but moved toward the door. "Are you cooking pizza tonight?"

"Of course."

He put his hand on the glass door and started to push it open. "Save me a seat."

"Sure." She watched him leave, moving quickly along the sidewalk and across the street. He walked like a man who had a lot of things to do. Things he didn't want to talk about. She turned back to the clerk and handed her the check, but she couldn't shake the feeling that something was wrong. Why was Peter so interested in 1963?

"WHAT IS TAKING so long?" Peter leaned forward, his corned-beef sandwich forgotten on the table. He'd driven to Spokane that afternoon, determined to find out exactly what the investigation had turned up so far, determined to talk to the detective in person, maybe even do a little investigating on his own. Anything to speed up the whole process.

Mike Morelli looked more like an aging prizefighter than a successful private detective. He lit another cigarette and took his time answering. "Look, I told Mrs. Johnson that this wasn't going to be simple. I don't even have the birth mother's name, and no one in Hope seems to remember the girl Mitch Parkins was in love with thirty-one years ago."

Or they weren't going to say, Peter thought, remembering the mayor's reluctance to talk about the past.

Mike slid a manila envelope toward Peter and inhaled deeply before blowing smoke out of the side of his mouth. "Here's a report on everything I've got so far, including an updated list of the girls who gave birth to babies that would have been conceived that summer. Trouble is, some of the names are pure fiction. The good news is that I also have a list of names of couples who were waiting to adopt the babies."

"But no way of matching them?"

He shook his head. "The place has been closed for more than twenty years. I've been working from the birth-mother angle. I'm locating them, asking if Mitchell Parkins was the father of their baby."

Peter swallowed. "You're doing *what?*"

Mike's expression softened. "Look, it's the only way. And I'm careful not to upset them. So far, I've tracked down eight of them—thank goodness for computers— and all of them denied being in north Idaho that summer."

"And when you reach the right woman?"

"I'll ask her if she knows who adopted her child, if it was a boy or a girl, and if she recognizes any of the names on the list of adoptive parents. I also ask them if they remember any of the other girls who lived there, if they talked about their past or their boyfriends."

"I'll try to find out who the girl was," Peter said. "I've been to the newspaper office and the library and made copies of anything that might hold a clue."

"Good luck. You have connections there, which will help," Mike said, smashing his cigarette into the ashtray. "I've got to quit," he muttered. "My daughter keeps after me about my bad habits."

"What about the birth certificates?"

Mike shook his head. "That's tricky. It takes a court order to unseal the original records. And unless your thirty-year-old mystery child has already researched his or her past, we don't have much of a chance of getting at confidential records. The next step is locating those thirty-year-olds, just in case one of them has done all this work for us." He grinned. "We might just come across the one who knows exactly who his birth parents were." He stood, brushing cracker crumbs from his khaki slacks. He held out his hand. "Keep in touch, Pete. You work your angle, and I'll keep tracking down these names." He nodded toward the stack of paper. "Keep going through those," he said. "I didn't come across anything obvious when I read those old newspapers, but you might notice something I didn't."

"All right."

Mike hesitated. "Anything else on your mind?"

"One of the names. Jane Plainfield."

He nodded. "The one you told me not to contact."

"Yeah. You're sure she's one of the babies?"

"Her parents' names are on the list of adoptive couples. According to the records, they adopted a baby in

April of 1964, a baby who would have been conceived in July of 1963."

"And Jane is their only child."

"Right."

Peter ran his hand through his hair. "Guess that answers my question."

"Look, son, you don't have to get involved in this if you don't want to. Digging around in people's lives is never—well—nice. It's messy, and it's not a job for everyone." He gestured toward the manila envelope on the table. "Forget it. I'll send a copy to your stepmother, so she knows she's getting her money's worth, and you go back to Hope and catch a big fish."

"I wish it were that easy," Peter said, picking up the envelope and his papers. "But it's not. Not anymore."

Mike didn't look at all surprised. He dropped a ten-dollar bill on the table to pay for their lunch. "Then you're involved with the Plainfield woman?"

"Yes." Peter nodded, wondering what Jane would think if she knew he was snooping into her past. "A woman who could get hurt."

"I don't think your stepmother considered that when she started this investigation."

Peter walked beside him to the door. "Neither did I."

"Take some advice, Pete. Back off this case or give up the woman. Doing both doesn't work."

He didn't want to accept the wisdom of those words. "The odds are she's not Ruth's niece."

Mike stopped at the door and shot Peter a sympathetic smile. "Do it your way, then. Just don't be surprised when it blows up in your face."

JANE GAVE UP ON HIM the third day. By Wednesday night, when he didn't join Don and Linda at the café for a steak dinner, she decided Peter Johnson and his sexy brown eyes had returned to Boise. To flirt with other women, no doubt. Smart women who didn't take him seriously.

She couldn't ask Don where his houseguest had gone without looking as if she'd been dumped. And she didn't want anyone to know she cared, although Denise kept giving her sympathetic looks whenever they were between orders.

By Friday morning she'd slid into self-disgust and renewed resolve to avoid men. Especially those who gave her boats and picnics and kisses and compliments. Peter Johnson had been a fun diversion, but he'd lasted about ten days. Then he and his mysterious "research" had ridden off into the sunset.

Well, now it was time to get back to normal. Peter could walk in here this morning and she'd act like nothing had ever happened between them. As if she'd never been tempted to invite him into her house and keep him there until dawn. After all, she decided, picking up the coffeepot, she had her pride. She'd stretch her legs and refill coffee cups and take a break from the heat of the grill. Maybe she'd even take a few days off, she mused, heading toward the front tables.

The bell on the door jangled as Peter walked in and practically knocked her down. She managed to hang on to the coffeepot without spilling any of its contents down the front of her apron. He gripped her shoulders to steady her.

"Hey!" His smile never wavered, despite her embarrassed expression. "You're just the woman I wanted to see." He glanced at the carafe in her hand. "What are you doing away from the grill?"

"Helping Denise." She stepped sideways and he dropped his hands. She wouldn't ask where he'd been all week, she vowed. It was none of her business, and he didn't need to know she'd missed him.

"I'm glad I made it back for the weekend," he said, following her to a table. "I didn't know—"

"Hey, Pete! Over here!" Don Stone waved from a corner booth. "What did you do, drive all night?"

"I got in early this morning," he said, hesitating before joining Don in the booth. Jane tried to hear Don's next question, but the bell jangled again and masked his words. She hid a sigh of frustration, torn between being glad to see Peter again and disgusted with herself for the jolt of excitement she'd felt when he touched her.

Denise hurried around the corner. "I'll do that," she offered. "I just had to call home and make sure Angela knew that Robbie had a swimming lesson this morning."

"That's okay." Jane didn't relinquish the pot. "I'll finish making the rounds if you want to start washing dishes. I think the breakfast rush is over."

Denise checked the clock. "There should be one more wave of customers before ten."

"I hope you're right," Jane replied, knowing that being busy would keep her mind off the man in the corner booth.

Jane heard the noise first, as she refilled coffee cups at the front table to the left of the door. Not exactly an explosion, she realized, but more a crash. "What—"

People looked around, wondering at the loud bang they'd heard outside, then Jane turned to the side window in time to see a large yellow dump truck careening toward the building. She froze, still holding the coffee carafe, and tried to warn everyone.

"Get out," she managed, but her voice wasn't loud enough to be heard. She stood, stunned, as yellow filled the picture window, and waited for it to crash through the cement blocks and run them all down, but nothing happened. She waited for long seconds, then slowly turned to the rest of the people in the café.

"Did you see—" she began, but every other person in the place stared out the front windows at the highway, where clothes fluttered to the asphalt and part of a truck bed tumbled across the white line and stopped a few feet from the Open for Breakfast sign on the edge of the parking area. It looked like a garage sale had exploded, as several pots bounced onto the gravel and rolled down the slight incline.

A split second of silence followed as Jane, too, stared out the window.

"What in hell—!" someone exclaimed.

"The driver?"

People jumped up, scraping back their chairs from the tables and heading toward the door. Jane turned back to the west window to see if she had imagined the giant yellow dump truck, but it was still there. Or at least, yellow metal still gleamed on the other side of the glass.

She felt strong arms around her, and the carafe was removed from her hand and set down on a nearby table.

"I need to call an ambulance," she said, wondering why Peter thought she needed his support.

"I will," he cautioned, holding her against him in the empty café. Only a couple of minutes had passed since the men ran out of the restaurant, but she could hear their shouts.

Don opened the door and stuck his head in. "You won't believe this," he said.

"I'll call an ambulance," she repeated, trying to duck away from Peter's arm.

Don shot her a sympathetic look. "There's no need. We—"

She felt her knees give way, but Peter grabbed her before she could slump to the floor. "They're *dead?*" She looked past Don to the wreckage that was strewed over the road. The pickup must have been filled with camping gear and the cap that covered the truck bed had flown off at the impact.

"No," he hurried to assure her. "We found the driver. He was thrown out of the truck. He'd fallen asleep at the wheel, and landed in the grass. He's a little stunned, but he's okay. And he was the only one in the truck."

"Thank God," Peter said. "What happened?"

"You've got to come out here and see it to believe it," Don told her.

"I have to call the police," Jane insisted. "And there's a big yellow—"

"I'll do it," Don offered. "You two go look on the side of the building."

Jane stopped, urging Peter to look toward the left. "That's what I'm trying to tell you," she argued. "There's a dump truck over there."

Peter stared at the window. "What is a state dump truck doing against your building?"

Don strode over to the phone. "Go outside and see how lucky you are, Jane. I've never seen anything like it."

Peter took her by the hand and led her outside. Tim stood at the side of the building, his hands on his hips. "P.J.!" he shouted. "Come over here!"

Jane really didn't want to look. She expected to see crumbling cement. And bodies. And blood.

"Open your eyes," Peter told her. "It's perfectly safe."

She did, and understood what had prevented the enormous truck from smashing through her wall: two cars parked along the side of the restaurant, Roger Cantrell's 1979 Cadillac and Mark Price's new van. Roger and Mark stood staring, as if they still couldn't believe their eyes.

Tim pointed toward the highway. "The truck was parked up there, on the side of the road. And it was towing a roller."

"A roller?"

"One of those machines that rolls asphalt smooth," Peter explained.

Tim nodded. "Some guy fell asleep at the wheel, coming home from Seattle, I heard. Anyway, he fell asleep, went off the road and hit the roller. The roller bumped the truck, just enough to send it rolling down the hill toward the café."

Jane looked up at Peter. "That's what I saw, the truck rolling toward the window."

"You *saw* it?"

"I was facing that way when I heard the crash."

"Why didn't you run?"

She shrugged. "I don't know. Now I know what people mean when they say they were 'frozen to the spot.'"

His arm tightened around her. "You were lucky you weren't killed."

"We all were," Tim said. "If that pickup truck had hit the gasoline pumps in front of the café, we'd all be blasted to bits right now."

Jane turned wide eyes to Peter as the sound of sirens filled the air. "Really?"

He put a comforting arm around her once again. "Don't think about it."

"Here come the police," Tim stated unnecessarily. "Wait till they get a load of this!"

Jane turned toward the restaurant and saw people drifting through the door, Denise right behind them. "I have to go back to work."

"No, you don't," Peter countered.

She pulled away from him, willing her shaking knees to support her without Peter's help. "I have to. From the looks of things, everyone in town is going to be drinking coffee and talking about this accident for the rest of the morning."

She moved away from him, determined to ignore the urge to put her head onto his chest, wrap her arms around his waist, and burst into tears.

7

"I'M FINE," JANE insisted, picking up the spatula and examining the breakfast order Denise had clipped to the hood of the grill.

Peter took his customary place at the counter, on the end stool. "You've had a shock."

"Yes, well, the police can take care of it. And no one was hurt, so we can go on with the day."

"Take the rest of the day off," he insisted. Denise plopped a cup of coffee in front of him without asking if he wanted it and scurried off. Jane turned and looked at him as if he'd suggested she fry eggs on top of her head. He tried again. "Take the day off and get out of here."

She put her hands on her hips, the spatula forgotten as it rested on her apron. "And exactly how am I supposed to do that? I don't have another cook coming in until tomorrow."

"Put a sign on the door that says Closed for the Day, and walk out." Peter took a sip of the coffee. He was glad he'd been able to point out the obvious solution.

She jerked her thumb toward the door. "Out."

"What?"

"You can leave any time. I don't have time to stand here and argue. Three more state troopers just drove up and everyone in town is going to come down here to see what happened. There'll probably be tow trucks, too.

And in another couple of hours people are going to start wanting lunch. I don't have time to stand here and listen to ridiculous things like, 'Put a sign on the door.'" She shook the spatula at him, and a piece of egg yolk landed on his shirt.

Peter stood, picked up his coffee cup and backed away before any more garbage could hit his white polo shirt. "I'll go find Don and have breakfast, but I'm not leaving." He turned as the door opened and let in more curious townspeople, then shot her a parting glance over his shoulder. "I'll be here if you need me."

She'd need him, he decided. Especially if she was right about everyone in town coming to the restaurant. Denise looked as if she needed roller skates already, and her yellow ponytail was at half-mast.

"Who's waiting for breakfast?" Jane called to the crowd. "I can't remember what I've cooked and what I haven't, so if you're waiting for something to eat you'd better come up here and tell me about it!"

Peter grinned to himself as he slid into the booth across from Don. Didn't anything fluster that woman? He remembered her expression the morning after the barbecue and knew that there was one thing that shook her up.

"What are you smiling about? Escaping death by explosion?" Don looked outside at the police cars scattered across the parking lot. "They're out there talking about what would have happened if that truck had hit the gasoline pumps. No one can believe how close we came to blowing up."

"Or being crushed to death by a state dump truck." He took a sip of his coffee. "I didn't know they made trucks that big."

Don chuckled. "Have you eaten?"

Peter shook his head. "I don't dare order anything, either. She's mad at me."

"You were gone almost all week. She probably thought you'd left for good."

"I tried to call her a couple of times, but didn't get any answer. I should have called the café, I guess, but I didn't think she'd appreciate being interrupted at work."

Don lowered his voice, despite the high volume of conversation all around them. "Did you find out anything more?"

"Not much. I did a little exploring on my own, though. And the detective let me tag along with him. I think he felt sorry for me."

"Tag along where?" Don leaned forward.

"To a couple of interviews with the women who'd been at the home in Spokane that winter. We thought we were on to something for a while, which is why I stayed. I kept thinking that one more day might mean the answer, would mean finding Ruth's niece or nephew and I'd be off the hook."

Denise paused at their booth. "You two want breakfast?"

"I already ate," Don said. "But Peter here could use something."

"The usual?"

He shook his head. "Something easy," he said. "A couple of scrambled eggs and a side of bacon."

Denise scribbled on her pad. "White toast, right?"

"Right. Thanks."

She grinned at him. "Where've you been all week?"

"Missed me?"

"Not me. Someone else around here, though." She started to move away, but Peter stopped her.

"You mean you think there's hope for me?"

She shrugged. "I don't know, Peter. She's been hurt once before, really bad. Maybe she's not ready to take another chance."

"Denise!" Jane called. "Your order's up!"

"Coming!" She winked at Don and hurried away.

"This is all very interesting," Don drawled, taking a napkin and wiping a puddle of coffee from under his cup. "But what are you going to do if you can't find Ruth's relative? You can't stay in Hope forever."

"That's true." Peter picked up his coffee and glanced over at Jane. Her dark curls were tied at the nape of her neck, but several had escaped and stuck to her cheek and forehead. She wiped her hands on her apron and took another carton of eggs from the refrigerator. She was stubborn and independent, and yet he couldn't stay away from her. "But when I leave, I don't intend to be alone."

SHE WISHED HE'D GO away. She didn't need another body taking up space in the already crowded room. Every seat was filled, and practically every coffee cup was either being used or sat piled on the counter by the sinks. Silverware was soaking in hot water until Denise had a chance to wash it. When Jane saw Peter stand and Don leave, she fought a battle between disappointment and relief.

Both feelings were short-lived, because Peter headed to the counter instead of the door.

"What can I do?" he asked. He looked a little nervous when she picked up a handful of ground sirloin and rolled it into a ball.

She decided to take him up on his offer. "You can wash dishes."

He nodded, and came around the counter. The sinks were in the corner, tucked behind the soda machine, and he hesitated in front of them. "Any special instructions?"

"There's an apron hanging up behind you and rubber gloves on the shelf under the sink. Keep the water as hot as you can stand it and do the silverware first." She stopped, realizing she sounded like a marine drill sergeant. "And Peter?"

"Hmm?" He pulled the apron over his head and looked for the strings to fasten it around his waist.

"Thanks."

He smiled at her, and her stomach flipped over. He had the most startling ability to turn her into a blithering idiot. "You're welcome."

He worked faster than she thought he would. Somehow she hadn't expected him to know how to wash dishes, but he didn't seem to have any trouble. When the clean dishes piled up he'd grab a dish towel and wipe them dry, then start over again.

Denise raised her eyebrows when she saw him, but thankfully didn't make any comments. A few of the customers asked him if he couldn't pay his bill, but almost everyone else was too busy to pay much attention to P.J.'s new dishwasher.

She was right about the crowd. It was going to be a record-breaking day when she counted the receipts tonight. She wriggled her aching toes. That is, if she survived until tonight.

"Can you close early?" Peter shouted over the clatter of the dishes.

"It's Seafood Night. I advertised it in the paper." She flipped three burgers before adding, "I have extra help coming in, so I'm hoping for a big crowd."

"I guess that's a no."

"Yes." She thought for a moment, remembering the odd way he'd acted in the newspaper office. "How's your research coming?"

"My research?"

He was concentrating on scrubbing a plate, so she couldn't see his face. "What you were doing at the newspaper office," she prompted. "How is it coming?"

"Well . . ." Peter paused. "It's not as easy as I thought it would be."

Denise came over and helped put lettuce and sliced tomatoes on the plates that were waiting for hamburgers. "What are you researching?"

"Some family history," he answered. "My stepmother's family."

Jane grew even more curious. "Did she live around here?"

"A long time ago."

"In 1963?"

Peter gave her a sharp look. "Why did you mention that year?"

"I thought I heard you say something about that in the newspaper office."

"Where do you want these plates?" he asked, pointing to a stack of clean white dishes.

"I'll put them away," Denise offered. "You just stay right where you are."

"What about tomorrow?" Peter called out.

Jane checked the remaining orders. "What about tomorrow?"

"Can you take the day off and go up to the mountains with me? It's probably too early for huckleberries but I'd like to get some pictures of the view from up behind town."

Denise answered for her. "She can take the whole day off. Muriel can come in early and Callie and I can handle anything that comes up."

"It's your day off," Jane protested.

"I don't mind picking up the extra money," Denise admitted. "I'm saving for that food processor, remember? I'll close up for you at five."

"So, what do you say?" Peter's gaze held hers. He had soap bubbles up to his elbows and perspiration dotting his forehead, and he was the sexiest man she'd ever seen.

Jane sighed. She knew when she was beaten. After today, she'd like nothing better than to escape to the mountains and forget the café ever existed.

"All right," she said, telling herself she was foolish for looking forward to being alone with him.

"I THINK THIS IS AS FAR as we're going to get." Peter guided the Jeep into a clearing made by an old logging operation. The dirt road, a series of steep switchbacks up the side of the mountain, dwindled into a footpath.

"That's fine with me." She waited for him to turn off the engine before she hopped out. It was good to get onto solid ground. She'd felt a little queasy during the last couple of turns, especially when Peter had had to back up twice in order to make the turn. Visions of tumbling down the mountainside had flashed into her mind, so she'd closed her eyes and hung on to the seat, pretending she was sitting in her father's old leather recliner.

She reached back into the car for her backpack, hung the binoculars around her neck and put on her Seattle Mariners baseball cap while Peter fiddled with his camera.

"If we follow the trail we should find the top of this mountain. Don told me there's a lake behind here somewhere."

"Round Lake," Jane said.

"Once we get to the top we can hike along the ridge for as long as we want." He took the knapsack from her and hoisted it onto his back.

She followed him to the National Forest Service marker, up the trail, and after twenty minutes hiking, they entered a wide meadow dotted with high stalks of bear grass, its bushy yellow heads moving in the breeze. It was a familiar spot, with huckleberry bushes just beyond the clearing. "We're almost to the top," Jane murmured, inhaling the pine-scented breeze. It had been too long since she'd been up here; she hadn't realized how much she missed it.

"Look up," he said, and when she obeyed he snapped her picture. He grinned as she made a face at him. "I realized I didn't have any pictures of you."

"Give me your camera," she said. "I'll get a picture of you with the lake in the background."

"Good," he replied, doing as she said. "I'll have it enlarged for my office."

She listened to his instructions on how to focus the camera, then took two pictures of him standing in the clearing, his worn jeans and plaid shirt making him look as if he'd lived in a log cabin all his life.

"Why are you smiling?" he asked, finished with posing and approaching her.

"You don't look like the president of Baysider Boats."

He looked down at his scruffy hiking boots and worn jeans. Then he looked at her, eyeing her equally old boots and washed-out jeans. "And you look like you've done this a hundred times."

Jane grinned, knowing her red checked shirt had seen better days. "My father and I used to hike up these mountains a lot. I'm sure he'd always hoped for a son, but he made do with me. He taught me how to build a fire, fly-fish, and set up camp. I drew the line at hunting, though. To my mother's great relief."

"You mean there's something the invincible Jane Plainfield doesn't do?"

She frowned, stung by his words. "What's that supposed to mean?"

He took her hand and led her toward the National Forest Service trail marker. "It means that you're the most independent woman I've ever met. You don't like being told what to do and you don't like accepting help. You don't even like to admit you *need* help. Invincible," he declared. "Or at least, that's what you want people to believe."

"And you don't?" She didn't mind holding his strong hand, especially since there was no one to see it.

"No." He stopped and looked down at her. With his free hand he tilted the brim of her cap away from her forehead and caressed her cheek. "I don't believe it at all."

"I can take care of myself," she declared, resisting the temptation to hold his hand against her cheek and savor the warmth of his skin on hers.

"I'm sure you can," he whispered, his eyes dark and no longer teasing. "But don't you ever wish you didn't have to? At least, not all the time?"

His lips came dangerously close as she searched for an answer to his questions. "I don't have much of a choice," she managed, and then his lips met hers. He dropped her hand, and grasped her waist to pull her close against him.

Jane didn't realize she'd wound her hands around his neck until she felt his soft hair under her fingertips. She was on her toes, and he almost lifted her off the spongy ground as he kissed her. The same dizzy, heated feelings swept through her, weakening her knees and her resolve.

His tongue teased her lips, and she opened her mouth willingly, needing more of him to sample. He tasted of mint and coffee, and his tongue made delicious love to hers until Jane wondered if she would self-destruct from pure pleasure. His fingers gripped her waist and tugged her down to the earth with him, cradling her against his body.

She lay on top of him, her hair curling across his cheeks as she lifted her mouth from his and smiled. "We're not hiking."

He smoothed his hands lower, to the swell of her buttocks. "This is more fun."

She planted tiny kisses along his jawline. "I agree with you," she murmured, enjoying the freedom to explore his face with her lips.

"You agree with me?" There was laughter in his voice as he lifted the hem of her shirt and smoothed her bare back with his hands. "That's a first."

"Umm." She found his earlobe and nibbled softly. "Enjoy it for now."

"I will," he said, moving his hands higher to the line of her brassiere, then back to her waist in a soothing caress.

She liked the way she fit along his body but knew it couldn't be comfortable for him. She started to move away, but his hands held her still.

"Where are you going?"

"I was afraid I was hurting you."

His fingers dipped inside the waistband of her jeans. "Oh, I'm in pain, all right, but I'm getting used to it. It happens every time I'm around you." Peter grinned at her embarrassed expression. "You're blushing again."

"I can't help it." She held herself very still, conscious of his arousal against her thigh.

"One of these days I'm going to make love to you."

She shook her head, envisioning her naked body tangled with Peter's. It couldn't be as good as she imagined it would be. And making love with Peter would only commit her further to the relationship. She didn't want to fall in love with him, but she was afraid she was already halfway there. "No."

He didn't look convinced. "Soon," he countered. "For now, I'm going to kiss you for, say, another thirty or forty minutes."

"You are?"

"Sure. I finally have you all to myself, even if you've started arguing with me again. I'm going to make the most of it."

"At least you're honest."

"I try," he admitted, reaching to twine one of her long curls around his finger. He cupped the back of her neck and pulled her mouth down to his. She didn't know how long they lay there, kissing and touching and caressing, but when she lifted her head for air, her shirt was unbuttoned, and so was his. Her lace-covered breasts brushed against his chest and his lips were tickling her collarbone while his fingers worked at the front clasp of her bra.

Releasing her breasts, he rolled her over onto her back and smiled down at her. He smoothed the palm of one hand over her breast and cupped it in his hand. "So soft," he whispered, bending to kiss the rosy tip.

"Peter—" She started to protest, but her breath caught in her throat as sensation pulsed through her. It wasn't fair that he could do this to her, she decided. He touched her and she lost her clothes and her good sense.

He kissed his way to her other breast and duplicated his caresses before looking up at her. "Do you like this?"

"Too much," she admitted, wanting to cover herself. Sensing her withdrawal, he lifted himself off her, but didn't move from her side. Jane hooked her bra and buttoned her shirt with shaking fingers. The feelings he aroused in her were too complicated to be examined. She didn't want to come to depend on him or love him. She knew she was better off being alone. But the words sounded hollow, even though she only spoke them to herself.

"Should we hike to Round Lake and have lunch?" His voice was carefully casual.

"As long as we keep our clothes on," she replied, relieved by the easy tone in his voice.

"Well," he said, hauling himself to his feet. "I will if you will."

JANE AND PETER STOOD side by side and looked at the expanse of secluded mountain lake before them. Hot and sweaty, tired and dusty, they looked longingly at the cool blue water.

"I'll bet it's cold," Jane ventured.

"Think so?" Peter dropped the pack and wiped his forehead with his sleeve. "I didn't bring a suit."

"Neither did I." He turned to her, his lips starting to curve upward. "Don't even think it," she told him.

"We could wear our underwear."

Jane felt the perspiration snake between her breasts. She was hot and dirty and would love nothing more than to dive into the water and rinse off. "You won't look?"

"Of course, I'll look."

Jane sighed.

"Or we can skinny-dip," he suggested. "I'll leave the camera in the backpack."

"Kind of you."

"Well, I'm a nice guy." He began to unbutton his shirt.

"What are you doing?"

"Going swimming." He shrugged out of his shirt and tossed it on the grassy slope. "Don't stare."

"I'll do my best to resist," she answered.

He sat down and untied his boots, pulled off his thick socks and stood again to unzip his jeans. He pulled off the jeans and turned to her and winked. "I'll keep my briefs on, but if you decide you want me, just yell."

She couldn't help laughing at the expression on his face, but when he walked away from her she studied his wide back and the smooth expanse of skin above the elastic waist of his briefs. His legs were long and well-shaped and carried him quickly to the edge of the lake. He waded in quickly, and with a shout made a shallow dive underwater. She watched as he sputtered to the surface and brushed his hair out of his eyes.

He waved to her. "Come on! What are you waiting for?"

She felt like an idiot, standing on the shore while he was having all the fun. "All right," she said, unbuttoning her shirt. She'd leave her bra and underpants on, and try to get into the water as quickly as possible. After all, powder-blue cotton bikinis were not sexy lace-trimmed silk. He'd seen her in her bathing suit before, after the boat regatta, so what was the difference?

The difference, she decided, feeling very uncomfortable, was that she wasn't used to walking around in her underwear in front of Peter Johnson. It was the quickest striptease in the history of Idaho. Jane held her shirt in front of her until she reached the shoreline, only dropping it at the last minute. The water was like ice, and she paused, caught between self-preservation and embarrassment. Peter rose to the surface and studied her with a long, hungry look that made her next move easy: She dived, screaming as the cold enveloped her.

When she rose to the surface, she gasped for air. "You, you should . . . have t-told me!"

"And ruined the fun? No way." He ducked as she tried to splash him, laughing as she shivered. "Come here and I'll warm you up."

"Come h-here and I'll d-drown y-you!" She moved her arms and legs, hoping the action would warm her. She took a couple of deep breaths and kicked her feet, beginning to grow accustomed to the chilly temperature.

Peter ignored her threat and swam closer. "Feels good, doesn't it?"

"I'm not sure." She noticed he didn't come within arm's reach. She flipped over onto her back and floated, looking up at the cloudless sky.

"This is the life, isn't it?"

She looked at Peter floating beside her, sharing her view of the sky. "Yes."

"Is that an eagle?"

Jane squinted at the large bird circling a tall red fir. "It could be. Have you see the herons yet?"

"On the road to Clark Fork, in the slough?"

She nodded.

"Yes. But I still haven't seen the moose in Pack River yet."

"You will," she assured him, as if he were going to stay in town for the rest of his life. She didn't want to think about how much she'd miss him when he left. They floated side by side in the crystal blue water, the sun heating their exposed skin and the surface of the water, until Peter flipped over.

"I'm going in."

"Okay."

She almost forgot what she was wearing—or not wearing—until she followed him out of the lake, and saw the expression in his eyes when he turned back to speak to her. No sound came out of his mouth as his gaze traveled down her body to linger on her breasts, then dropped lower before returning to her face again.

Jane quickly bent and grabbed her shirt from where she'd dropped it on the shore, then held it in front of her.

"It doesn't matter, you know," Peter said, his voice low.

She eyed him curiously. "What?"

"I'd want you if you were wrapped in a coat from your neck to your toes." He smiled with a lopsided expression that made her chilled skin tingle. "You don't believe me?"

"Not really," she admitted. "I don't understand, Peter. Why me?" She turned slightly and slipped on her shirt, grateful for its warmth. "And I'm not being coy. Just curious."

He put his hands on her shoulders and turned her to him. "I don't have one answer, Janie. I was attracted to you from the first moment I saw you at the barbecue. I wondered if you had a date, and when you didn't seem to, I waited until I could approach you and ask you to dance." He brushed his mouth across hers. "Maybe it was your smile. Or your laugh. Or the way you felt in my arms." He dotted kisses along her jawline and down the column of her neck. "You make a great omelet, too."

"I've never had a response like this to my cooking." The familiar heated reaction to his kisses began low in her belly and radiated outward.

He lifted his head and smiled down at her. "You're a woman of many talents," he declared. "And you look good in your underwear."

"Thank you."

"I don't suppose I could convince you to take it off?"

She shook her head. "Let's eat lunch instead."

He ran his hands down her arms, rubbing the fabric to warm her. "You'd better finish putting your clothes on. If you want to eat lunch."

She eyed his bare chest, dark and appealing and very masculine. She didn't dare look lower. "You, too."

Jane turned away, grateful for the long shirttails that hid her behind as she made her way to the shade under the fir trees where they'd dropped the backpack. She didn't really want to eat lunch. She wanted to feel Peter's warm body against hers, inside her, enveloping her with his warmth.

Making love to him would be pretty damn good.

Jane grabbed her jeans and struggled to put them on over her damp skin, telling herself she was an idiot. A fool. The silliest woman in the state of Idaho, when it came right down to it.

It didn't matter that she'd tried her best to ignore him. Or that she didn't remember much of that tugboat ride, except a pleasant haze. Or that she'd done everything she could think of to make him go away. And that she'd missed him when he had.

She'd done something really stupid. Dangerous, even.

She'd fallen in love with Peter Johnson.

8

SHE'D PRETEND HE WAS one of her customers. A friend, nothing more. *I am with a friend on a picnic.* Jane handed him a roast-beef sandwich and tried not to let her fingers touch his. Physical contact was definitely not safe.

"Thanks," he said, completely unaware of her inner turmoil, thank goodness. "I'm starving."

Jane sighed, trying not to think of how she'd felt in his arms. Maybe three years without sex had distorted her thinking processes. Maybe she wasn't really falling in love with this man and it was a celibate's mirage.

She unwrapped her sandwich and eyed it with little enthusiasm. She'd never heard of a "celibate's mirage." The thought of being in love had ruined her appetite.

"What's the matter?"

Jane looked up. "Nothing," she fibbed, setting the sandwich on her lap and reaching into the backpack. "Root beer?"

"Sure."

She set the can on the grass in front of him before pulling out a plastic bag filled with sliced carrots and celery sticks and another bag filled with chocolate-chip cookies. "Help yourself."

"You're not eating," he observed, popping the tab on the can of soda. "Why not?"

She took a bite of the sandwich, chewed and swallowed. "Yes, I am."

"You still want to hike the ridge, don't you?"

No. I want to go home and hide in my house until you go back to Boise. She opened her soda and took a long swallow before answering. "Sure," she told him. "I'm looking forward to it."

"I should be able to get some great pictures."

She nodded her agreement as she bit into the sandwich.

"Unless you want to stay here and swim," he added, with a decided twinkle in his eyes.

She shook her head. "We're going to keep our clothes on from now on."

"Just during lunch," he teased.

"We'd better keep hiking."

She watched as he demolished the thick sandwich, half of the vegetables and three cookies. He finished the drink, set the can on the grass and leaned back in the shade of the fir trees.

"What happened to hiking the ridge?" she reminded.

He put his hands behind his head and closed his eyes. "I'm resting up. Besides, I have to think of some other way to get your clothes off you."

She couldn't help laughing. "Swimming in the mountain lake isn't going to work twice."

Peter kept his eyes closed and sighed with obvious contentment. "I'll think of something," he assured her, then was silent. She watched his breathing slow, noted the soft rise and fall of his chest as he napped under the trees.

It was easier to eat now that he wasn't looking at her with those knowing eyes. Easier to swallow without the lump in her throat. The food tasted better without the butterflies in her stomach and the distracting pounding of her heart. Jane shook her head, wondering how she'd let herself get into this predicament.

The boat, she realized, leaning back against a tree and spreading out her legs in front of her so that the grass tickled the bare soles of her feet. It had all started when she won the damn boat: For better or worse, Peter Johnson had been part of the prize.

She'd owned the damn thing for two weeks, although it seemed like a lot longer. Jane reached for a cookie. She wished she knew what to do with the boat. If only her father would return. This business about being all alone was starting to get on her nerves.

The rest of the day passed quickly and, to Jane's relief, it was easy to pretend Peter was simply a friend. The frequent times he'd grabbed her hand to help her down a slippery slope or up a rough pathway it had been easy enough to ignore the jolt of warmth that flowed between them at the physical contact.

By the time they returned to the Jeep, they were both hot, tired, and dusty, but Jane felt invigorated by the hours away from the responsibility of the café and the marina. She hated to admit it, even to herself, but yesterday's accident had left her more shaken than anyone would have realized.

Peter unlocked the car door and put his camera on the seat. "I should have brought more film."

Jane tossed her pack into the back seat. "I never saw anyone take so many pictures in my life. What are you going to do with them?"

"I want plenty of reminders of this summer." He smiled at her. "I'll see that you get copies of the best ones."

"I'd like that." She climbed into the Jeep and fastened her seat belt.

"You don't have to work tonight?" He turned the key in the ignition and guided the car onto the dirt road.

"No."

"Let me take you out to dinner. Something fancy."

"This is north Idaho," she told him. "There's no such thing as 'fancy.'"

"Don and Linda go to an Italian place in Sandpoint. It's supposed to be very elegant."

"Ivanoe's?"

He nodded. "That sounds right. Hang on," he warned, approaching the first difficult switchback. When Peter had safely negotiated the turn, he added, "They've asked if we'd like to join them tonight. Would you like to?"

When she hesitated, he continued. "Let me spoil you, Janie. Let someone else cook for you, for a change."

That was tempting. "Well . . ."

He sensed her weakening. "You can think of it as a professional duty. You know, check out the competition?"

She laughed, as he hoped she would. "Can I let you know when we get back? I want to make sure everything's okay at the marina before I leave it again."

He slowly let out the breath he'd been holding. He sensed time was running out. She'd deliberately withdrawn from him since that kiss at the edge of the lake, avoiding his touch except when she'd needed help along the path. But he'd accomplished what he'd set out to do, which was to give her a break from the hectic café so she could put the accident out of her mind.

The fact that he'd gotten her alone, all to himself, had been a bonus. And having her in his arms had been the grand prize.

"What time would you want to leave?"

"I'll call you. Probably around seven."

"Good." She sighed, leaning back against the seat. "That will give me time to do the books for the week."

Peter dared a personal question. "When's your father coming home?"

"Soon, I hope. He should call me this weekend. I need to ask him about the boat."

"Have you talked to him since you won it?"

"No. If I call him he'll think there's an emergency. And I hate to bother him."

"I'm sure he wouldn't think it was a bother."

She sighed, but he didn't dare take his eyes off the road in order to look at her. "I've been taking care of business for several years now."

"It's a big job for one person."

"Tim is a great help, but you're right. It *is* a big job."

He dared a more personal question. "Did your husband work at the marina?"

"Yes, although he always thought it should make more money and be less of a job."

Peter chuckled. "Obviously he'd never owned his own business."

"No. Turned out he married me for the marina and felt like he'd gotten a raw deal all the way around."

This time he looked at her. "He must have been crazy."

"Just ambitious. He thought he'd found his ticket to an easy life. Unfortunately it took me a while to catch on that I was being used."

"Did you love him?"

"Oh, yes. At first. I met him in college and he completely charmed me. I fell in love right away, certain I'd found the man of my dreams."

Peter winced at the bitterness in her voice and turned his attention back to the narrow mountain road. "How long were you married?"

"Five years." She looked out toward the lake. "Five very long years with a man who never stopped lying to me. It cost my father quite a bit of money to buy him off so I could divorce him without losing part of the business."

"And you've been divorced for three years?"

"Yes. Thank goodness." Her voice shook as she turned back to face him. "I swore I'd never get myself in that kind of situation again."

Peter sighed. He had a harder job ahead of him than he'd thought.

"ARE YOU GOING TO TELL me about it?"

"Tell you about what?" Jane dropped strips of bacon on the grill and stepped back to pick up her coffee cup. She'd been busy since they opened, with barely enough time to eat a piece of toast and swallow more than half a cup of coffee. Sundays were always busy, especially in the summertime, but today seemed more hectic than usual. Jane stared at the bacon and vowed to keep her mind on her work, and not daydreaming about her day on Lookout Mountain.

"Yesterday," Denise whispered, buttering toast for her order. "You know, the hike with Mr. Handsome. Dinner last night. Come on, you must have something to say about it."

"Not here."

Denise looked behind her at the counter where six men sat eating breakfast or drinking coffee. "No one can hear us. They're all talking about Bob Trimble's twenty-eight-pound Dolly Varden."

"Did you get a picture of it?"

"Of course, I did. It's on the bulletin board right now. Didn't you see it?"

Jane shook her head. She must be slipping. Too many late nights. Too many distractions. "I've had other things on my mind this morning."

"Like what?"

She shrugged. "I've decided to sell the boat. Dad may not be home for weeks and he hasn't called me."

"Call him."

"I don't want to interrupt his vacation with problems I can solve by myself."

"He wouldn't mind. You don't have to do everything by yourself."

Jane arranged the food on the two plates Denise had prepared, and turned her attention back to a large order of French toast while her friend delivered the breakfast order.

"My feet are killing me this morning." Denise leaned on the counter and made a face at Jane. "John and I went out on the town last night. We haven't danced like that in years."

"Thanks for taking over yesterday. I didn't get to tell you how much I appreciate it."

"I enjoyed being the boss," Denise admitted. "Muriel does a great job on the grill as long as I'm careful writing up the orders."

"She hates your handwriting."

"I know. She tells me often enough." Denise poured herself a cup of coffee. "Now, tell me about Peter."

"We had a good time." Jane remembered the way she'd sprawled across him in the bear grass and felt her cheeks grow pink.

Denise eyed her carefully. "I'm sure you did. Did you make love?"

"Shh!" Jane turned around to make sure no one was listening. "Denise, for heaven's sake!"

"I'm your best friend," she declared, not at all perturbed. "If you can't tell me, who can you tell?" She waited, her blue-eyed gaze fastened on Jane's face. "You did, huh?"

"No." She flipped the bread over. "I thought about it, though."

"Well, who wouldn't?" Denise sighed in exasperation. "Anyone can see you're crazy about each other."

"I've decided not to see him anymore."

"Are you nuts?" Denise grabbed her arm and hauled her into the pantry. "What are you doing?"

"Burning breakfast," Jane replied, edging toward the door. But Denise barred the way.

"I can't let you ruin your life."

"I'm not ruining anything," Jane argued, wishing she could say it with more conviction. "I just don't know if he's my type, that's all."

"Not your type?" her friend echoed, disbelief written all over her face.

"No."

Denise crossed her arms over her chest. "Exactly what *is* your type, then?"

She shrugged. "I'm not sure. Just that Peter isn't it."

Denise studied her for a long moment. "You're in love with him and you're scared to death."

"Right." Jane's eyes filled with tears. "What if he's just another charming schemer? I don't know anything about him, really. Except he's a friend of Don's and he owns a boat business."

"Ask Don."

"I can't do that. It seems so sneaky."

"I thought you had dinner with him last night. Did anything personal come up?" She took a paper napkin from the package on the shelf and handed it to Jane.

"Not really."

A male voice cut through the clatter of dishes. "Hey, P.J.! Something's smokin' out here!"

Denise swore under her breath. "Well, you'll just have to find out more about him. Besides the fact that he likes kids and can wash dishes and looks at you with those sexy eyes."

Jane wiped her eyes and headed back to the kitchen. "There's more to a relationship than that."

"Yeah? Like what?" Denise grumbled behind her.

Jane hurried over to her burning French toast. She couldn't think of a reply.

"NO, I HAVEN'T TALKED to him." Peter held the phone up to his ear and looked out the window. He never tired of the view of the steep Monarchs on the other side of the lake. "Why did you ever move away from this place, Ruth?"

He listened to her reply—something about falling in love with a traveling salesman before she met Peter's father. Then, before she could launch into another discussion of the merits of the private detective, he asked about Baysider. He knew full well that his stepmother and his plant manager could run the place without him, so it was no surprise to hear there was nothing pressing that needed his attention. The changes he'd made on the design of the stairs on model 31A were working out fine.

He promised, for the seventh time, that he would call Mike Morelli for an update. He promised he would call tomorrow. He promised he wouldn't go fishing if it looked like there was a storm coming up. He told her he missed her—which was true—and told her to stay off her hip and take good care of herself, and no, he didn't need anything. And yes, he was getting plenty to eat.

Peter chuckled when he hung up the phone. His attraction to a cook meant he'd gained three pounds. Ruth had nothing to worry about where his health was concerned, it was his heart that was in danger.

And his peace of mind. He couldn't continue to deceive Jane much longer. He wanted to make love to her, and he would—soon. He wanted her to trust him but he hadn't yet told her the truth about why he was in Hope. And he hadn't broached the subject of adoption, either.

Life would be simpler if Ruth had never found those old letters. But then again, he wouldn't have come to Hope and discovered the woman he'd been waiting all his life to meet.

"THE BIRTH MOTHER'S name was Lily."

Peter grabbed a pencil and a pad from among the papers piled on the kitchen table. Mike's call this afternoon had caught him outside on the balcony watching Linda feed the ducks that gathered by the dock for their afternoon snack. "How'd you find that out?"

"It was a pretty good lead from one of the other women who lived at Potter House at the time."

He wrote "Lily" at the top of the page. "No last name?"

"Not yet. But she gave birth to a girl sometime in April. The woman I talked to had her baby March thirty-first, and when she left a few days later, Lily was still pregnant. Their babies were due about the same time."

"A girl," he repeated. "How did she know that?"

"She didn't, but another woman I talked to did. So you can scratch off all the boys' names on that list I gave you."

"Just a minute." Peter found the list and frowned. *Chet and Ethel Plainfield, daughter Jane, born April 9, 1964, no other children.* He'd highlighted that entry, but there were nineteen others. He scanned the names of the couples who had adopted babies from the Spokane home that spring and crossed off those who'd adopted boys. "That leaves eleven possibilities."

"Three," Mike countered. "I've been able to eliminate every couple except Matteson, Kominski and Plainfield. Have you had any luck finding out anything about the Plainfield woman?"

"No. The subject hasn't come up."

"Don't worry, then. I'll go back through the newspapers and see if there's anything about someone named Lillian or Lily. Maybe we'll get lucky and find a last name."

Peter eyed the stack of papers on the table. "What good will that do?"

"I can find her, if I have a last name. None of the names on the list from the home fit, so she must have used an assumed name when she went there."

"You're sure about all of this?"

There was a moment of silence. "Yeah. You pay me to be sure."

"Well, keep me posted."

Mike chuckled. "You pay me for that, too."

"Don't send anything directly to Mrs. Johnson. I'll fill her in."

"You sure?"

"Positive," Peter declared. If Ruth knew that her missing niece might be in Hope, there'd be no keeping her quiet in Boise. And he didn't need any more problems while he was trying to convince Jane that he was the man for her.

"Fine. I'll be in touch."

Peter hung up the phone and eyed the stack of copied newspapers. The summer of '63 was piled up before him. He'd gone through it before, but not with the name "Lily" in mind. He took the stack of papers and moved outside to the shaded balcony. Mike could make his own search; but if there was anything in the local newspapers that connected someone named Lily to north Idaho, he wanted to be the one to find it. That was the only way he could protect Jane.

He didn't know what he wanted to protect her from, but if she was Ruth's niece, she deserved to hear the story from someone who loved her.

Peter hooked his feet on the railing and leaned back in the chair. Maybe it was a little early to use the word *love*, but he knew deep in his gut that what he felt for Jane—since almost the first moment he saw her—could last a lifetime.

Hours later, Peter glanced at his watch. Almost dinner, and time for one of the café's big burgers and an order of French fries. He eyed his flat stomach. On second thought, maybe he'd skip the fries today. He'd finish the paper and head over to flirt with Jane for a little while.

He smiled at the memory of Saturday afternoon and Jane's reluctance to swim in her underwear.

She'd looked pretty incredible in her underwear.

He turned his attention back to the page on his lap. Once he finished this he could head next door. So far so good. There'd been no mention of anyone named Lily, although he'd come across a photo of Chet Plainfield holding a derby-winning fish in April. He'd studied the grainy photo of Jane's adoptive father and wondered how the man could have left his daughter in charge of such a time-consuming business. Didn't he care about her? Did he realize how hard she worked?

Martha McPherson also has company this summer. Her goddaughter, Lily Simmons, is visiting from Missoula before starting college at the University of Idaho in the fall. Martha's husband, Jeb, reports that her gallbladder surgery went well and they are looking forward to a trip to Vancouver in October.

Peter looked back up at the heading on the column: Hope and Clark Fork Community News.

Lily Simmons. A teenager visiting in the area during the summer of 1963. Probably to help her godmother recover from surgery. Had she fallen in love with a young local man? Had Mitchell Parkins made her pregnant before his boat tipped over on the lake? She must have been devastated and terrified when he died. Had Martha McPherson dried Lily's tears and driven her to Spokane?

He looked at the remaining names on the original list of adoptees. According to the best private detective in the Northwest, Lily had given birth to Kelly Matteson, Eve Kominski or Jane Plainfield. He sure as hell hoped it wasn't Jane, because every day he spent in Hope meant he wasn't telling her the truth.

He had the uncomfortable feeling that Jane wouldn't appreciate the deception. He put his papers down and decided to head over to the café. If he didn't know better, he'd think Jane had been avoiding him. Maybe tonight he could talk her into taking time for a evening boat ride and a swim.

"I CAN'T," SHE DECLARED, her dark curls swinging against her cheek as she bent over to grab something under the counter. He watched as she dropped a handful of forks onto a tray and turned away from him.

"Why not?"

She waved her arm around the room. "I can't get out of here early. This is a birthday party. I'm up to my elbows in pizza, and I have to finish putting the buffet together."

He looked around, realizing why the place was so packed on a Monday evening. "All these people are Roger's friends?"

"Most of them. I can't close the restaurant completely, but since I serve mostly local people anyway, it doesn't really matter. The birthday guests are on one side of the room, and I've kept a couple of booths on the other side for tourists. Mary, Roger's wife, didn't mind, as long as she surprised him."

"And did she?"

Jane grinned. "She sure did. Too bad you missed it."

Denise moved over to the soda dispenser. "He thought he was stopping to put gas in his car. You should have seen his face!"

Peter twisted around on his stool and surveyed the crowd. Several men waved to him. "Looks like the regular breakfast crowd."

Jane poured herself a glass of water. "I'm surprised Don didn't tell you about it."

"I've been busy." *Busy trying to figure out if you're Mitchell Parkins's daughter.*

Denise set drinks on a tray and turned to leave. "Do you know what you want, Peter?"

He grinned at Jane, who chose to ignore his raised eyebrows. "A hamburger and fries and . . . I want Jane to go out on the lake with me tonight."

Denise picked up the tray and winked at Peter. "I'm afraid I can't help you, although I've tried."

"I told you, I can't," Jane replied, picking up the long-handled spatula.

"Sure, you can."

"No."

"I want to talk to you about the boat."

"I've decided to sell it."

"I've decided to lease it."

She turned from the grill. "What?"

"It's the perfect solution," he stated, wondering why he hadn't thought of it sooner. "I'm going to be here a while longer and I'd like access to a boat." He grinned. "Especially one I designed." He could see that she didn't mind the idea.

"All right. I have a standard lease contract I can give you."

"Good. By the way, when is your birthday?"

"April ninth. Why?"

Just as Morelli said. "Just wondering."

"When's yours?"

"October twenty-fourth. Will you give me a party?"

Jane chuckled. "You won't be here in October."

He took her hand as she stepped up to the counter. "You never know what can happen in a couple of months, Janie." He dropped her hand and slipped off the stool. "I'll go wish Roger a happy birthday. Come over to the cabin when you're finished here and I'll pour you a glass of wine and we'll talk about the boat, all right?"

"You'll go away and let me get back to work?"

He wished she hadn't phrased it quite that way. "Yes," he agreed, wondering what else he would have to promise to get her to be alone with him.

"I could be late."

"It doesn't matter. I'll leave the porch light on." She still didn't look convinced. "If you don't say yes I'll think you're avoiding me." Her cheeks flushed, and he knew it wasn't from the heat of the grill. "Are you?"

"Of course not," she snapped, but a guilty expression crossed her face.

"Good." He tried not to smile, tried to look businesslike and not do what he wanted to do, which was take her in his arms and kiss her until she dropped her spatula. "I'll see you later."

"Later," she echoed. He could barely hear her over the noise of the crowd, but he thought she added, "I must need my head examined."

9

JANE RAN HER FINGERS through her drying hair and hoped she didn't look too tired. Taking a quick shower had helped, but her feet still burned from standing at the grill for the past four hours. She locked the door of her trailer and stepped out into the cool night air.

The parking lot was finally empty, its streetlamp shining on the gas pumps and lighting her way across the pavement to the Rainbow Resort. To Peter Johnson's cabin.

She wished she didn't like him so much; wished it was simple physical attraction and nothing more. But it wasn't. She liked his sense of humor, his easygoing manner and the way he protected her.

Even when she didn't need protecting.

She liked the way his dark hair curled against the nape of his neck and the way his long fingers curved around a coffee mug. She liked the way he kissed and the way he walked and the way he enjoyed his meals.

She liked a man with an appetite.

Jane hesitated as she approached the end cabin. A light shone on the porch, just as Peter had promised it would. She took a deep breath and clutched the papers in her hand. *Strictly business,* she assured herself. No reason for her stomach to flutter or her steps to quicken at the thought of seeing him.

No reason, except that he stood in the doorway watching her cross the wooden porch, and he opened the screen door wide to beckon her in. "I wondered if you were coming," he declared, his voice low. He wore a white sweatshirt and a pair of black bathing trunks.

"It took a long time to clean up," she informed him, stepping inside to the cozy pine-paneled room. "Have you been swimming?"

He let the door close behind her and followed her into the tiny living room. "Yeah. I couldn't resist one last swim before the sun went down. Have a seat."

"Thanks." She sat down on the tweed sofa and put the papers on the pine coffee table. "Here's the information on the lease. It's pretty standard."

Peter ignored the papers and went over to the kitchen area. "I'm glad you came." He took two wineglasses from the cupboard and opened the refrigerator. "You'd like a glass of wine, wouldn't you?"

"I shouldn't stay long."

He hesitated as he set the wine on the counter. "Is that a 'yes' or a 'no'?"

She felt like an idiot. Why on earth was she so nervous all of a sudden? Because she was on his territory, for a change? This was ridiculous.

"A 'yes,'" she declared, hoping she sounded casual and relaxed. She made a conscious effort to lean back against the couch.

He stepped around the corner and handed her the glass. Then he took the chair across from her and set his own glass on the coffee table before picking up the papers. He scanned them and tossed them back on the table. "Looks fine to me. It sure solves both our problems."

"Yes, it does." She took another sip of the wine, enjoying the pleasant warmth it produced. She kicked off her sandals and curled her bare feet underneath her, determined to act as if she leased boats to handsome tourists every night. And drank wine while doing it.

"I'll sign these before you go."

"Fine."

"Want me to do that?"

Peter looked at her feet, and Jane realized she'd been rubbing her sore toes with her free hand. "Of course not," she began, but he moved to the end of the couch.

"Lean back," he ordered. "And stretch out. Put your feet in my lap."

"Peter—"

He grinned. "Haven't you ever had a foot rub?"

"No." She set her glass on the table and wondered if she should leave.

"Every cook should," he declared, setting his glass next to hers. "I like those shorts."

She looked down at her baggy white cotton shorts. "Why?"

He grinned, and took one foot in his strong hands. "Because I get to look at your legs. You have great legs."

"I do?" She would have protested, but at that moment his thumb moved against the sole of her foot, massaging a sore spot. Any objections she would have made faded as he massaged the bottom of her foot with strong fingers. She leaned back against the arm of the couch and offered both feet willingly.

"Feel good?"

"Umm." She closed her eyes and tried not to moan aloud. He took her other foot and placed it on his thigh so he could rub both at once. She sighed with contentment as he eased the soreness in her feet and toes. "How did you learn to do this?"

"I didn't," he replied, laughter edging his voice. "But you have to admit it was a good way to get you to lie down."

Visions of other women resting their aching toes on Peter's hard thigh annoyed her, and she opened her eyes to see if he was teasing.

He grinned, and she tried to move. "I thought you were being nice."

He held on to her ankles so she couldn't get up. "I am," he insisted. "This is no seduction, Janie. I just thought it would feel good to you."

"Really?" She leaned back again.

"Really," he declared. "I've never rubbed anyone's feet until yours."

She ignored the amusement in his voice, decided to believe him, and closed her eyes. He gently pulled each toe until she moaned with pleasure. "Don't stop."

"I'm not," he said. "I'm taking a sip of wine."

His fingers resumed their magic on her feet until the tension in her body eased and she lay on the couch like a piece of overcooked spaghetti.

"Feel better?"

"Umm." She wriggled her toes and stretched her legs. "Do it some more."

He caught her feet in his hands to stop her. "Careful," he said. "Your heels are perilously close to my—"

"Sorry!" Her eyes flew open, and she jerked her feet away and planted them on the cushion. Then she struggled to sit up. "I didn't mean—"

He leaned forward and gave her a hand, tugging her

into a sitting position. "I know," he said, trying not to laugh. "But a man can't be too careful." He kept a gentle grip on her hands.

"I think I'd better—"

"Because," he continued, as if she hadn't interrupted him, "I intend to make love to you tonight, and getting kicked in the groin would put a damper on my plans."

She couldn't think of one single objection, and that shocked her. Surely she could come up with a good reason to leave this room, this cabin. This man. Jane looked down at her hands, held firmly in Peter's, and her toes tingled. "I can see how it would," she agreed, looking back up at him.

His mouth came very close to hers and Jane lifted her chin to meet his kiss.

"You're not leaving?"

She inhaled the faint scent of his after-shave and felt her willpower dissolve. "I haven't decided yet."

His lips brushed hers, then curved up at the corners. "Let me know when you've made up your mind."

"Okay."

He released her hands and she twined them around his neck, then met his lips with hers in a heated kiss that threatened to topple her backward. She loved kissing him, loved the warmth of his lips and the feel of his hands holding her shoulders and the way his mouth slanted at just the right angle against hers.

The passion that rose between them was no different from the first time; was different only in that she knew him now. Knew he was the kind of man she could fall in love with—if she hadn't already.

His hands dropped to her waist and tugged her closer to his hard body. Her legs brushed his bare thighs as she fell backward on the couch. He lay on top of her and lifted his mouth from hers.

"Brings back memories, doesn't it?"

She frowned. What on earth was he talking about? "Memories of what?"

"Our tugboat ride." He rubbed her lips with the pad of his thumb. "You shouldn't glare at me like that."

"I don't remember much about that night," she admitted, running her fingers through the soft waves at the nape of his neck. "Except I think I enjoyed it."

"You *think?*"

She nodded, enjoying the way he lay on top of her, his elbows propped to take his weight. It was so good to feel a man's body against hers once again. Three years was a long time.

"Believe me, sweetheart, you didn't have any complaints."

She pulled his head toward hers. "Come here." The kiss continued for long, endless seconds. She couldn't breathe and she didn't want to. She just wanted to feel him parting her lips with his tongue, delving into the recesses of her mouth to tease her and please her.

He slowly released her mouth. "Changed your mind yet?"

"Still thinking," she murmured, touching her lips to his. "Are you in a hurry?"

He sighed, his breath fanning her lips and sending little shivers along her spine. "No," he whispered. "I could make love to you all night long, so there's no hurry at all."

"All night?" she echoed.

He trailed kisses along her jawline toward her ear, and Jane thought she'd melt right into the couch. "Uh-huh."

She bit back a groan. "You're not making this easy."

"I don't want you to leave." He lifted his head and looked down at her with dark eyes.

Jane touched his face in a loving caress. Was it already too late to turn back? Despite her best intentions, her heart had been given before tonight. And, no matter how hard she'd tried to deny it, Peter Johnson was part of her life now. At least for this moment of time. She looked into his eyes, seeing the passion in his gaze. She wasn't fool enough to believe he was really in love with her.

"I've wanted you since the first minute I saw you," he said. "Sounds crazy, doesn't it?"

She nodded, and ran her thumb along his upper lip. He had beautiful lips.

"Every time we're together I have trouble keeping my hands off you," he admitted.

"Why are we like this?"

Peter knew the answer. "Because we're right for each other."

She didn't smile. "How can you be so sure?"

He looked down into those gorgeous eyes, felt her soft body beneath his, and knew with overpowering certainty that this woman was meant to be his. "I've never been more sure of anything in my life."

"Sure enough for both of us?"

He shook his head. "No. You have to want me as much as I want you or this won't work."

"All right," she whispered, caressing his cheek. "It's probably crazy to want someone this much, but I do."

He stared down at her, wondering if he'd heard correctly. She met his gaze, her lips slightly swollen from his kisses. He liked knowing the flush on her cheeks was caused by passion.

"It's inevitable, you know." He bent to kiss her again, only this time the kiss was possessive in its intensity. He wanted her to know that she was going to be his.

"I'm starting to believe you," she replied when he lifted his lips from hers.

"Good. That's the first step."

"What's next?"

He grinned, liking the way her mouth turned up at the corners when she teased him. "Are you in a hurry, Ms. Plainfield?"

"I'm nervous," she said, giving him a lopsided smile that tore at his heart. Peter raised himself off her and stood, giving her a hand as she sat up. Tousled and flushed, she'd never looked more desirable.

"Come," he told her, keeping her hand and tugging her toward a pine door.

Jane hesitated in the doorway of the dark room. She didn't want to rush. She wanted to savor every moment, because after she and Peter had made love, everything would be different. They could never go back to the way things were before.

"Is something wrong?"

She shook her head. "No. I was just wondering how this would change things between us."

He put his hands on her shoulders and kissed her. Then he smiled down into her eyes. "Nothing could change the way I feel about you."

And how is that? But she dropped her gaze and didn't voice the question. She didn't really know if she wanted to hear the answer or not, and she knew he'd be truthful. He'd never lied to her, thank goodness. She felt the soft brush of his hands along her back, lifting the hem of her shirt and sliding underneath, along skin that suddenly tingled with awareness.

The only light came from the living room—a dim glow that infiltrated the bedroom's darkness and outlined the furniture. Three steps brought them to the double bed that took up most of the room. Jane's nervousness dropped away as Peter touched her. It seemed natural to tumble together across the mattress, to take each other's clothes off in a hasty tangle, to kiss and caress each other's bodies in the cool darkness.

Somehow it felt right, Jane realized, wondering how the awkwardness had disappeared. She wanted nothing more than to make love to this man, this man who seemed to adore her body as if he actually thought she was beautiful.

That was the biggest surprise of all.

When she reached for him in the dark, Peter hesitated before sliding closer to her, and she realized that up until this minute she hadn't thought of the necessary precautions. Not having a sex life had its advantages: you didn't have to worry about disease or pregnancy.

"Wait," he said, reaching into the drawer of the nightstand. "I almost forgot."

"I'm glad you remembered," she whispered. "I'm not used to thinking about . . . that."

"Come here," he whispered, lying on his side to face her. She turned to look at him, moving closer so their lips met easily. She ran her fingers down his shoulder and across the crinkly hair on his chest and loved having the freedom to enjoy his body. She moved the palm of her hand across his hipbone, then lower still, to the hard shaft that felt smooth and hot to her touch.

"I like touching you," she murmured, before his lips claimed hers. He held the back of her head with one hand, keeping her close to him, while the other hand was free to roam her body. He nudged her onto her back, which allowed his fingers intimate access. She pulled him down on top of her, wanting only to have him inside her.

He took her then, moving her thighs apart with his knee, touching her with his erection, thrusting gently inside her welcoming warmth. Jane closed her eyes and touched his waist as he filled her. When he possessed her fully, he held himself still and bent down to take her lips with his. Their breath mingled as again he moved slowly within her.

When he lifted his head and looked at her, Jane smiled, wondering at the pleasure she felt from having him inside her. Peter kissed the corner of her mouth; she caressed his face.

"I intend to do this all night," he declared.

"Good," she barely managed to say, because he moved within her again, taking her breath away.

Much, much later, he held her face between his hands and watched her expression as tremors shook her body. He knew he'd never seen anything so beautiful. Groaning, he could no longer hold back his own climax and shuddered within her tight warmth for long, sweet moments.

Jane held him to her, until he moved onto his side, taking her with him. He brushed the curls from her forehead and tucked her against his shoulder.

"Comfortable?"

"Stunned," she admitted. He was still inside her, and her body still trembled from the intense climax.

"Me, too."

They rested together in silence for a few more minutes. He stroked her hair while she closed her eyes and wondered what had just happened between them. They'd made love, of course, but there was more to it than that. She was in love with him, she knew. And he cared for her; of that much she was certain.

It would have to be enough.

"STAY," PETER DEMANDED, reaching for her as she attempted to slide out of bed. He grasped warm female skin, the smooth dip of waist between ribs and hip, and stilled her flight from him.

"I can't," she whispered, but she lay back down and turned to face him in the darkness.

"Of course, you can." He didn't want her to leave. Not now. He had the feeling she would disappear if he let go of her; would return to her home, and in the morning at the café she'd pretend they'd never made love. Or never even met.

"I shouldn't," she replied, snuggling back under the covers. He pulled the light blanket over her shoulder and ran one finger down her breast to its rosy peak.

"Of course, you should," he told her, dipping his head to the warm skin beneath her ear.

"I have to get up in . . ." She peeked over his shoulder to the alarm clock resting on the nightstand. "Three hours."

"Stay here."

"And walk across the parking lot in the morning? No way."

"Go around the other side," he suggested, lifting his head and smiling into her eyes. "I'll help you. If we run into anyone we'll say we went out for a sunrise boat ride."

Jane snuggled deeper under the covers. "All right," she murmured, as he pulled her against him. "Just this once."

Peter hesitated. He wanted many more nights with this woman, not "just this once." He started to argue, but Jane's soft curves molded to his body, making speech impossible. Besides, how could he convince her of his feelings without scaring her away?

"WHAT ARE YOU DOING?"

Jane jumped, grateful for Peter's grip on her hand. It took her a second to recognize Tim's voice, but by the time she turned, she realized her chief mechanic must be nearby. Dawn was breaking, but the morning light hadn't lifted the darkness enough to reveal anything but the largest outlines of the buildings.

"Oh. Hi." She hoped she didn't look guilty. It was none of Tim's business, anyway.

Tim stepped out from the corner of the shop. "What's up?"

"Nothing much," Jane answered. "Heading to work."

"We just came back from a boat ride," Peter offered, sounding amused. Jane squeezed his hand, hoping he'd be quiet.

"Oh?" Tim ignored him, concentrating instead on Jane. "Must have been some boat ride."

Jane nodded. "Well, see you later. I have to get the coffee started and the grill heated up. You know how it goes." She tugged Peter's hand, hoping he'd get the message and move toward the café.

"Wait," Tim said, stepping forward. "I have a message for you. From Chet."

"Dad? Is everything okay?"

"Yeah. He just wanted you to know he'd be home next week, and everything was fine. He'd been trying to reach you for hours, so he called me, just in case you were at Denise's house or in Spokane shopping or something."

Her heart sank. "He must have been worried."

Tim shrugged. "Not really. I said everything around here was fine." He looked over at Peter and frowned. "I didn't tell him anything more than that."

"I'm looking forward to meeting him," Peter said evenly.

"Yeah, well, I bet he'll want to meet you, too." Tim turned back to Jane. "He sounded fine. Said he had a good trip and he'd try to call you later on, today."

"Thanks, Tim. I appreciate it. He didn't say what day he was coming home?"

Tim shook his head. "I don't think so, P.J."

"Well, thanks again."

"Yeah. Anytime."

Jane tugged Peter toward the front of the restaurant, then quickly dropped his hand. She'd forgotten she'd been holding on to him like a lovesick teenager. "Thank goodness the parking lot is empty."

"What difference does it make if anyone sees us? What are you so afraid of?"

"I don't like my private life discussed in the café."

"Why not?" He stood back as she fiddled with the keys to find the right one. "They discuss everything else in this place."

She unlocked the door and pushed it open, then flicked the light switch with automatic movements. "Yes, well, my husband and my divorce were pretty hot topics around town, and I never want to go through that again."

He followed her as she crossed the restaurant and stepped behind the counter to the grill. "I can't picture anyone being mean to you."

"They weren't." She flipped another set of switches and the fluorescent lights flickered, then came on with a sudden burst of brightness. "Everyone was full of sympathy and advice."

He frowned. "What's wrong with that?"

Jane shook her head and grabbed her apron. "A little goes a long way. Would you fill the coffeepot with cold water? Just pour it in the top and I'll do the rest." She turned on the grill and took the potatoes from the refrigerator. If she didn't get the hash browns on first, she'd be in trouble. That, and the bacon and sausage. It always paid off to get them started, shove them to the back to keep warm, then finish cooking them to order.

"What time do people start coming?"

"Around six, or when I turn the outside lights on." Jane tossed the premeasured coffee into a filter and tucked it into its holder, then switched on the machine. "Denise will be in around six-thirty. I manage the early birds by myself."

"I'm sure you do," he murmured, coming up behind her and wrapping his arms around her waist. Jane fought the urge to melt against him and let him nuzzle her neck—something he was clearly attempting with those very skilled lips of his. The hours in his bed and in his arms were all too vivid, and she felt her cheeks flush. She'd loved making love with him.

"We can't do this," she managed to say. The hiss of the coffee splashing into the carafe almost disguised her words.

"We're not doing anything," he countered, his breath warm near her ear.

"You have to leave."

He released her, turning her around to face him. "Why?"

"So no one sees you here first, before I open up." Jane almost laughed at the look on his face. "You can come back later," she assured him. "Go get some sleep."

He grinned. "You don't want me around because it's obvious what we've been doing all night. It's written all over your face."

Jane shook her head, but she couldn't help smiling at him. "Yours, too."

"Let me stay," he coaxed. "I won't look at you."

"You'll distract me and I'll burn the toast and over-cook the eggs."

"And your customers wouldn't say a word," he added, but he moved away from her. "I'll see you later, then. What about dinner tonight? Can we go out?"

"It's a pizza night."

"What about a boat ride later?"

Jane knew she shouldn't agree. "Okay."

"Good." His gaze lingered on her lips, but he backed up a step.

"Use the back door. I'll unlock it for you."

He followed her to the door. "I'll see you later."

"I'll be here." The words held no comfort. She'd rather follow him out of the café and back to bed. Jane turned back to the grill and looked up at the clock. Something told her it was going to be a long day.

At least her father was coming home. But would Peter still be here to meet him?

Her father wouldn't think much of her summer affair. He believed in marriage and commitment and "till death do you part." He wouldn't understand a sexual attraction that could no longer be hidden, or her weakness for a man with twinkling brown eyes and an easy smile—and a way of touching her that made her insides turn to pancake syrup.

But there was no future for a boat designer from Boise, a city a twelve-hour drive away, and a cook from Bonner County. She had no desire to live anywhere else, and Peter's life revolved around his business.

As hers did.

She didn't know how she'd explain all this to her father, a man who believed that love was forever, not a temporary condition.

10

"YOU WANT TO GO *WHERE?*"

"To the base of the Monarchs," Peter replied, ignoring his plate piled high with eggs, bacon, hash browns and toast. "Don said it was a great overnight trip. I thought we could—"

"Your breakfast is getting cold," she interrupted.

He ignored her warning. "Go camping. It's a long way across the lake, but we could follow the shoreline so you wouldn't be afraid. It would take longer, but we'd get to the same place."

"The base of the Monarchs," she repeated. She looked out the window over the sink at the steep mountains that seemed to rise out of the lake to the south. She'd never spent any time camping at their base, but as a child she'd picked huckleberries with her mother on the high ridges, reached from behind by a four-wheel-drive truck.

Peter nodded. "We can camp there overnight and even do a little fishing. And swimming," he added. "Only this time—"

"I'll remember my bathing suit," she finished for him.

"That's not what I was going to say." He picked up a slice of toast and took a large bite.

"When?"

"I thought we'd leave early Saturday morning or even Friday evening, before dark. Can you get the time off?"

"I'm not sure."

He looked disappointed. "I don't want to force you, if you're really uncomfortable with the idea. I just thought it would be a fun way to be alone and use the boat."

"And you're right," she agreed. "I'll think it over."

"Great. We'll need camping equipment, but Don offered whatever he has."

"My father has plenty. We'll find what we need in the garage." She couldn't believe she'd almost agreed to this. Just went to prove what falling in love could do to a woman.

"Has he called back?"

"No. He'll probably just walk in here one day next week. He's like that."

"P.J.!"

Jane turned to see Denise waving an order slip at her. She slipped out of the booth and stood. "I'll see you later."

"I'll be back tonight, after dinner," he said, picking up his fork.

"You're not coming for pizza?"

He shook his head. "I'll wait for Steak Night. And I thought I'd do some fishing this afternoon."

"I'll see you later, then."

"Yes." His dark eyes crinkled at the corners as he returned her smile. "You certainly will."

"P.J.!"

"Coming," she called, reluctantly leaving Peter to eat his breakfast alone. She wondered what it would be like to be alone with him for several days, without the intrusions of her work, without interested customers watching their every conversation. It might even be worth going across the lake to find out.

"TAKE A FEW DAYS OFF."

Jane finished counting the steaks before she replied to Denise's suggestion. "Why?"

"You've been messing up the orders all morning." Denise sipped her coffee and then lowered her voice. "I have a good idea where your mind is."

"Stop teasing. Do we have another bag of French fries in the freezer?"

"No, but the order should be coming in any minute now."

"Good. I think I'm going to have to get more meat for tomorrow night. Last Wednesday we served forty-seven dinners."

"I couldn't believe how many people came in."

"Neither could I." Jane poured herself a fresh cup of coffee, relieved to have a break in the breakfast orders. The little bit of sleep she'd had last night wasn't helping her get through the morning. More caffeine might do it, though. "This time I advertised, but you never know what to expect."

"Speaking of not knowing what to expect, tell me what happened with our handsome Mr. Johnson."

"What do you mean?" Jane glanced over at the empty stools and realized no one was close enough to hear their conversation.

"Last night," Denise whispered. "You were going to his cabin to lease the boat. From the way you were looking at each other this morning, I'd say that you did more than talk about fishing."

"He leased the boat for the rest of the summer. Four more weeks."

"So he's planning to stay here all that time?"

"I didn't ask. Maybe he plans to come up on weekends."

Denise looked doubtful. "That's a long trip for the weekend."

"Not if you fly."

"True."

They each sipped their coffee, and Jane looked out the front window. Bob Trimble drove in, but headed down to the marina.

"You don't want to talk about it?"

"It was wonderful," Jane admitted. If she closed her eyes she could remember almost every detail. "Really wonderful. It's been such a long time since, well . . ."

"I thought Peter looked pretty cheerful this morning." Denise shot her a wicked grin. "Even though he didn't look like he got much sleep. He ate his usual breakfast but drank about five cups of coffee. And he couldn't take his eyes off you. The man has that lovesick look."

Jane shook her head. "Don't make more of this than it is."

"What is it, then?"

She shrugged. "Just something for the summer. Something very special, though."

"Well, make the most of it. It's always a long winter," Denise warned.

Jane set her coffee mug on the counter and stretched. She was tired of cooking, tired of frying eggs and burgers and fries. She was even tired of making pots of coffee and chatting with the same people day after day. "Maybe you're right, Den. Maybe I should take some time off."

Denise's face brightened. "Good! Muriel and I will work out a schedule with Cassie. We should be able to manage just fine. When?"

"Peter wants to go camping. I'll take off after Seafood Night, and not come back until Monday afternoon. Can you stay late and clean up for me Friday?"

"No problem. You sure that's long enough?"

Jane thought of romantic fireside conversations and snuggling in her sleeping bag, with Peter beside her. "It's perfect for what I have in mind."

"Then it's done," Denise declared. "I'll call Muriel and set everything up."

"Thanks." She was surprised at the relief she felt. To be able to walk away from the responsibility of the café was a luxury she hadn't experienced for the past two years.

She couldn't wait to tell Peter.

JANE LEFT DENISE in charge after the late-lunch crowd finished drifting in. She took a deep breath of fresh air as she stepped out of the café and looked up at the sky. A layer of gray clouds covered the sun, and the wind smelled like it was going to rain. She turned and looked at the lake, but the water didn't look choppy. It would be a good afternoon to crawl under the covers. Taking a shower and climbing into bed sounded better and better.

Jane looked at her watch. Two hours until she had to report back to work, seven hours until she saw Peter again. It was silly to feel this happy, she knew, but she couldn't help it. Silly, too, to feel lonely in the middle of a crowded restaurant every day, but since last night the empty space around her heart didn't hurt quite so much.

Jane unlocked the door and stepped into her quiet trailer. Tiny and insulated, up until now it had been the perfect place for her to escape to. She hadn't admitted she was lonely until Peter came into her life. He was pure male: strong, stubborn, protective and demanding. But he had a sense of humor, a sexy grin, and a surprising kindness that surfaced at the most amazing times. She was more attracted to him than she'd been to any other man, which was the scary part. Her ex-husband had also swept her off her feet in a whirlwind courtship that had left her breathless and infatuated and dazzled with love.

She hadn't realized until too late that Sean had planned the whole thing: to marry a wealthy college girl and set himself up in the family business. He'd lied to get what he wanted, and she'd been too starry-eyed to see through him.

Chet hadn't, though he'd tried to hide his misgivings and give Sean the benefit of the doubt. It hadn't taken long for the whole thing to fall apart.

Now, Jane realized, stripping off the clothes that smelled like grease, she was falling in love again. Only this time she was going to be more careful. Falling in love didn't have to mean a lifetime commitment.

Falling in love meant spending a weekend at the base of the Monarchs, roasting marshmallows and making love.

"THIS ISN'T EXACTLY the way I'd planned it."

Jane huddled under the blue tarp, her knees pulled up against her chest. "Me either."

"The weatherman just said something about 'light showers.'" Peter peered out of the shelter and looked up at the sky. "This doesn't look like 'light showers' to me."

"Have some more wine," she suggested, holding out the bottle. "It will warm you up."

"Good idea," he said, taking the bottle and holding it to his lips for a long swallow. They'd forgotten to bring glasses, and the coffee mugs were packed inside the boat. It wasn't worth getting soaked to find them. The rain had begun as they'd approached the narrow strip of beach. They'd barely had time to dock the boat at the shore and set up a temporary shelter before the rain started in earnest. "Are you hungry?"

"Not yet."

The food was still packed safely in the boat's hull. "Maybe this will let up soon." But Peter didn't believe his own words. The rain came down steadily, although no thunder or lightning accompanied it. They weren't in any danger, except from catching cold, he supposed. The dull drizzle was not the romantic setting he'd wanted for their time away together. He hadn't planned to spend Friday evening watching the rain. He turned to Jane. "This isn't very romantic."

She grinned at him. "At least we're alone."

"True."

"And we're not getting wet," she added.

He scooted back to sit beside her. "We can sleep in the boat if the rain gets worse."

"What about the tent?"

"We can set it up, I suppose, but we'll get wet while we're doing it."

Jane took the wine bottle from him and had a sip. "I don't care, as long as I don't have to cook."

He put his arm around her and held her tightly against him. "Are you warm enough?"

"I'm fine." She took another sip of wine. "I used to go camping with my parents."

"Tell me about your mother," Peter said, hoping she would say something like, *I inherited her temper and her way with pizza dough.* Something that would put to rest any remaining questions about Jane's connection to his stepmother.

Jane snuggled against him. "She was a lovely person, quiet and patient."

"Like you?" he teased.

"Very funny." They huddled together in silence for a few minutes. "What about yours?"

"Unfortunately I don't remember her very well. I'm very close to my stepmother, though. She's been a partner in the business for years."

"You don't mind?"

"Hell, no. I'm basically a designer, and Ruth's interest in the business helps me spend time at the drawing board. I don't know what I'll do when she wants to retire. Baysider has always been in the family."

Jane shivered, and Peter drew her closer to him. "Cold?"

"A little," she admitted. "Maybe this wasn't such a good idea."

"It's too dark to head back to Hope," he stated. "Unless you want to cut directly across the lake. Going around it would take a long time."

"I'd rather spend the night here."

"You sure?"

She nodded. "What if we were halfway across and the wind came up? Or there was lightning?"

"We'll stay here, then," he agreed. "As long as you don't mind getting wet. It could be a long night."

She turned her face up to his and smiled. "I can think of ways to keep warm."

"I'm stranded on a beach with a woman who wants to take advantage of me?"

"Yeah. Is that a problem?"

He bent down and kissed her, tasting the tart wine on her lips. "Not unless you expect me to take my sweatshirt off."

She wrapped her arms around his neck. "You can leave it on. Anything below the waist comes off."

Peter tugged his shirt from the waistband of his jeans. "I will if you will."

Jane brushed her lips against his. "It's a deal," she murmured. "Do you think making love will keep us warm?"

He moved the wine bottle to the corner of their shelter and spread out the sleeping bags. "There's only one way to find out."

"I like the way you think."

"I like the way you—"

"Shh," she whispered, putting a finger to his lips. "Why don't you show me?"

She didn't have to ask again. His fingers found the waistband of her jeans, and he caressed the warm skin above the fabric for long seconds before unsnapping the waist, lowering the zipper tab, and sliding his palm against the silk panties underneath the denim.

Jane mimicked his movements, her hands at his waist, until they managed to remove each other's clothing without knocking over the plastic shelter above them. A gray mist surrounded them, and the quiet drizzle of the rain, along with the slight lapping of waves against the smooth rocks, were the only sounds as they tumbled against the padded ground.

He heard her welcoming gasp when he entered her, and her hands caressed his back, pushing up the heavy fleece of his sweatshirt. She was tight and warm, surrounding him with the perfect fit of her soft heat. He moved within her, knowing that he had never felt anything like this before, certain that he would never find it again. Unless he made love to Jane.

She slid her hands lower, to touch him where their bodies joined. Peter leaned down to kiss her, and Jane moved her hands to his hips, urging him closer. He couldn't help plunging deeper, but he kept his movements slow. He wanted to feel every inch of her; he wanted her to feel every inch of him. When he heard her soft cry, felt the sweet contractions clutch him, he could hold back no longer. He came into her with hard, sure strokes until his shaking arms could no longer support the weight of his body.

When Peter found his breath, he rolled onto his side, taking Jane with him. The bulky shirt concealed her breasts, so he had to be content with nuzzling her neck until he felt her laugh.

"Am I tickling you?"

"Yes," she managed to say. She tilted her head back to look at him. Her hazel eyes sparkled, even in the last bit of remaining light. "But don't stop."

He carefully withdrew from her. "I have to, at least for now. If we're going to spend the night here, we'll have to make a better shelter and unload the boat." He stopped to look back at her. "Why are you smiling?"

"I like the way you make love," she whispered.

Peter kissed her on the lips before reaching for his pants. "Keep looking at me like that," he warned, "and we'll be sleeping under this thing till morning."

"Would that be so bad?"

He tugged on his jeans. "No. But I'd like to make love to you without worrying about water seeping into the sleeping bags. I was trying to give you a romantic evening," he said, wincing as the rain came down harder on the plastic cover.

"You just did."

"Stay here," he said, when she moved to find her underwear. "I'll take care of everything."

"You can't put up a tent by yourself."

"I've done it before."

Jane struggled to pull her jeans over her hips. She would have preferred to stay warm and half naked in Peter's arms, but if the man was determined to fix a shelter and find the food, then the least she could do would be to help him. She didn't want to return to Hope—not yet. It was too much of a luxury to have Peter all to herself, with no responsibilities and no curious eyes to watch and wonder if something was going on.

No, it was an easy decision to spend the night in Peter's arms, despite the rain and encroaching darkness. She'd brought a little propane stove, so they'd share a hot meal before climbing back inside a sleeping bag to make love again.

Jane smiled as she hurried out into the rain. It sounded like a night made in heaven.

"IF WE'RE VERY, VERY quiet we can sneak back to the cabin without anyone knowing we're here," Peter said, pulling the boat up to the dock in the stillness of early morning.

"Tim will know. He'll see the boat in the mooring and know." Which was fine, Jane decided. He'd know she was back safely.

"I talked to Don on the radio last night and told him where we were, and that we were going to stay put. He'll see the lights on at the cabin and know we're back."

Jane hesitated as she climbed out of the boat and looked toward the café. "Maybe I should just check in and make sure everything is okay."

Peter lifted the cooler onto the dock. "They've barely opened, Jane. What could go wrong in the past hour?"

"Well, maybe you're right."

"Come on," he ordered, keeping his voice low. "We'll get the rest of this later. I'm ready for a hot shower and a warm bed, aren't you?"

"Yes. And hot coffee."

He took her hand and tugged her across the parking lot toward the Rainbow Resort. Within minutes they were inside the small cabin, with the door locked behind them.

"See how much fun it is to be on vacation?"

It was the perfect opening for the question that had been on her mind. "And how long will that be?"

"I haven't decided yet."

He didn't sound happy about it, she noted, turning to see the briefcase on the kitchen table. "Are you still working on your research project?"

"No," he said. "I don't need to know anything more."

That seemed odd. She looked over at him, but he had turned to the sink to fill the coffeepot with water.

"You take the first shower," he offered. "I'll wait for the coffee."

"All right," she agreed, anxious to feel hot water on her damp skin. She was chilled to the bone, despite the fact that they'd made love twice, sleeping wrapped in each other's arms in cozy contentment. The trip back across the lake, taking the long way close to the shore, had chilled them both.

The bathroom was tiny, the metal shower stall old but clean. Jane took longer than she'd planned, letting the steaming water warm her skin until she felt drowsy and content. When she stepped out of the shower, Peter handed her a towel.

"I like this," he said, waiting for her to secure the towel around her body before handing her the mug of hot coffee. But Jane didn't ask him what he meant. She knew, because she felt the same way. This cozy intimacy was dangerous, she reminded herself, and seductive in its easy warmth.

"My turn," Peter announced, pulling the sweatshirt over his head. "You can wear one of my shirts if you want."

Jane slipped past him and headed toward the wide bed. For a few hours in that warm, dry bed she'd risk anything.

"I'M SURE IT'S HERE somewhere." Jane got down on her hands and knees and peered into the corner bookcase.

Peter admired the view of her bottom in tight jeans for a long moment. Only the memory of their long hours of lovemaking in his cabin this morning kept him from reaching for her. He wondered if he'd ever stop wanting her.

He didn't think so.

Jane turned, a triumphant smile on her face. "Got it!"

"Are you going to tell me what you've been looking for?"

She sat cross-legged on the floor, a heavy book on her lap. She flipped through the pages, pausing to peer at the pictures until he joined her on the plush carpet. Her father's house was dark except for the light in the corner shining on the pages of the photo album.

Jane pointed to the picture in the upper right-hand corner. "There. I knew I could find it. I've wanted to show you this ever since you mentioned camping in the Monarchs."

Peter looked closer. A young woman and a small girl stood displaying a bucket. "Is that you?"

"My mother and I picking berries on top of the Monarchs. That was a pretty exciting day for an eight-year-old."

"Let me see." Peter reached for the book. He told himself that he wasn't snooping, that it was perfectly natural to be curious about what Jane's mother looked like. He didn't see any resemblance at all, of course. Mike Morelli had said Jane Plainfield was adopted, so she must be. "You don't look like your mother," he commented, hating himself for baiting her.

"No. I was adopted when I was a baby," Jane informed him.

Peter didn't have to fake surprise. He hadn't expected her to tell him. "You've never mentioned that before."

She nodded. "It's not very important, I guess."

He swallowed. It was the only reason he'd come to Hope: because Jane Plainfield was adopted. "Not important?"

Jane shrugged. "It's hard to explain. I've seen those talk shows, where they reunite birth parents with the children they gave up for adoption, or adult adoptees are searching for their birth mothers, but I've never felt that way." Her smile was rueful. "I can't imagine my life being different than it is now, or having different parents."

"You've never felt the need to know where you came from?"

She shook her head. "Why would I want to meet the person who gave me away? Is that so hard to believe?"

He cleared his throat, afraid he would say the wrong words. Afraid he would say anything to hurt her and knowing he would rather his tongue fell out before doing so. "No. You must have had a very happy childhood." He turned back to the pages and pointed to a chubby child holding a fish. "Tell me about this one," he said.

"That's me," she said unnecessarily. "I used to fish from the dock." She turned page after page, explaining the photographs, sometimes replacing the ones that had slipped from their holders.

"Where's your father?" None of the pictures he'd seen included Chet Plainfield, and Peter was curious to know what Jane's adoptive father looked like. After all, he'd be meeting the man in a few days.

"He took the pictures," Jane said, laughing. "He loves to take pictures." She turned and pointed to a black-and-white photograph on the wall. "There he is with his second-place derby winner."

Peter looked at the framed picture on the paneled wall above the hearth. It was the same one he'd seen in the newspaper. "That's quite a fish."

"He was very proud of himself," Jane declared, shutting the album and tucking it back into the bookcase. "Come on. I'll get some steaks out of the freezer and make us some lunch."

"Steaks?"

"They're already cooked," she explained. "I just have to put them in the microwave and you'll think I just took them off the grill." She stood and dusted off her jeans. "I have to clean this place before Dad gets back," she muttered.

Peter forgot about the photographs and the steaks and the search for the missing niece when Jane looked at him. "Marry me," he said, surprising himself with the words.

"What?"

"Marry me," he repeated, liking the sound of the words. It was a brilliant idea, after all, and not completely unexpected. He knew already that he didn't want to live without her.

"Why?"

"Because I'm completely and totally in love with you," he explained, stepping forward to take her in his arms. "That's a good enough reason for me. How about you?"

Her voice was muffled against his chest, so he pulled back.

"Oh, I'm in love with you," she echoed, looking up at him with an expression he couldn't interpret. "But that doesn't mean I'm going to marry you. Or anyone."

"Why not?"

"We've only known each other a few weeks."

"I knew from the moment I saw you," he countered. "It was love at first sight."

"I don't think it happens like that."

"*Something* happened on that tugboat." His voice grew soft. "Then how *does* it happen, Janie?"

"You have to have time," she declared. "Time to be sure you're not going to make a mistake. Time to be sure you're not going to get hurt."

"And how much time is that?"

"I don't know," she whispered. "But I know I can't marry you . . . can't marry anybody."

He frowned, unwilling to let her go without having heard the answer he'd expected. A *Yes, my Peter, I'll marry you.* "I'll make you change your mind," he promised, then kissed her softly.

"Can I fix lunch first?"

Peter grinned and released her. "Absolutely."

11

"YOU REALLY SHOULD name her." Peter held out his hand and Jane took it to step into the boat. The skies had finally cleared, and he'd convinced her to take the sunset ride he seemed to have his heart set on. "You can't keep calling it 'the boat.'"

"Her next owner can name her."

"You still don't want to keep her?" He shook his head. "She's one of my best designs."

"Nothing personal," Jane assured him. "She's a lovely boat, and I've enjoyed her. I'm glad you're going to be using her, though."

"I'll name her, then."

"Go ahead." She followed him to the helm and took her place beside him as if she'd been doing it for years. She glanced over at him, wondering what he was thinking. They hadn't spoken of anything personal since he'd asked her to marry him three hours ago.

He'd asked and she'd said, "Why?" Jane closed her eyes briefly and wondered what on earth she was doing. She didn't want another husband. She didn't want to change her life. She didn't want this boat. She didn't want to answer to anyone.

And she didn't want to get hurt.

"The *Lucky Lady*," Peter announced. "What do you think of that name?"

She turned to him and wondered what these past weeks would have been like without him. Peaceful, no doubt. "It's certainly appropriate."

"You *are* a very lucky lady, you know."

"Me? I thought you were naming the boat."

"I am. But I'm talking about you. You won a boat at the barbecue and a prize at the boat regatta this summer. Have you bought any lottery tickets lately?"

She laughed. "No."

"Maybe you should." He started the engine, then guided the boat toward the open water of the bay. "If you're on a winning streak, you should make the most of it."

She didn't answer, knowing her words wouldn't be heard over the roar of the engine. She watched the shoreline instead, as Peter drove around the circumference of the bay before facing the western mountains and cutting the engine. He poured them each a glass of wine, settled cushions in the stern, and turned to wait for the sun to set behind the mountains.

Jane took a sip and watched the sky. She wondered if he'd ask her again, but hoped he wouldn't. There wasn't anything more to say, anyway. She had made up her mind a long time ago.

"YOU LOOK LIKE YOU LOST your best friend." Don joined Peter on the driftwood log and, like his friend, faced the lake in the dim morning light.

"I asked her to marry me."

"Jane?"

Peter turned to his friend. "You're surprised? I thought it was obvious."

"You've only known her a few weeks."

"That's what she said." Peter picked up a flat rock and aimed it at the water, then watched it skip four times across the calm surface.

"Give her time. From what I heard, her husband was a real bad character. She has the right to be a little gun-shy."

The two men sat in silence and watched the lake. Peter tossed another rock. "She told me she's adopted," he finally added.

"Do you think she's the one you've been looking for?"

Peter's smile was grim. "In more ways than one. I have to call the detective this morning and find out what he's learned. And I'm not too anxious to make the call. She's happy with her life as it is, and I don't think she'll welcome a new aunt...or a stepbrother. And I'm sure she won't appreciate that I haven't told her the truth."

Don skipped a stone along the surface of the water, watching it as it finally sank. "It's never too late," he noted.

"She might not be the one. If she isn't, then she never has to know why I really came here."

Don stood. "Come on. Let's go over to the café for breakfast. You can ask her to marry you again."

Peter joined him, stretching his cramped muscles. He hadn't slept well last night. "I'll be over later. I have some phone calls to make."

"How long are you going to stay?"

"Until she agrees to marry me."

"From the sound of it, that could take a while."

"Well, I'm not about to let her go," he admitted, giving Don a sheepish look. "It's taken me a long time to find this woman, and I'm not going to give up now."

"YES, RUTH. Don gave me all your messages. I just haven't had anything new to tell you." He hoped she'd believe the lie, but his stepmother continued to interrogate him about the detective's latest findings.

"I'm going to call him after I talk to you," he assured her. "But I need you to do something for me. Do you have a picture of your brother that you could send me? I'll give you Don's fax number or you can express it to me."

Ruth promised she'd fax the photograph as soon as someone could come out to the house and pick it up.

"How's your hip today?"

"I'm feeling fine," she assured him. "And I'll be even better once I meet Mitch's child."

Jane's declaration echoed in his head. "But what if the child doesn't want to be found?"

The silence on the other end of the line startled him. "Ruth? Are you all right?"

"I never thought of that possibility," she replied, her voice breaking a little. "Do you think that could happen?"

Peter hesitated. He seemed to be telling a whole pile of lies this summer. "I doubt it, Ruth. But you have to admit, it's a possibility."

"I can't imagine any such thing," she declared, sounding stronger. "Why wouldn't anyone want to know the truth about themselves?"

Peter could think of a lot of reasons, but he kept them to himself and promised to call if there was any news. For the rest of the phone call they discussed Baysider and the latest sales figures. He thought he'd made it safely through the call until Ruth, ready to hang up, said, "You're not telling me everything, Peter Johnson, and don't think I don't know it."

"Ruth—"

"No," she interrupted. "Don't even try to wriggle out of it, whatever it is. You think you're pulling the wool over my eyes, but you're not. I'm not senile, you know."

Peter chuckled, knowing how capably his step-mother ran Baysider. "You're a lot smarter than I am."

"I won't argue with you on that one," she sniffed. "But the next time we talk, you'd better have some answers for me. About a lot of things."

"All right," he promised. "I'll call Morelli and talk to you again as soon as I know anything more."

He could tell she wasn't convinced. Thank goodness she wasn't able to make the trip to Hope, otherwise he and Mike Morelli would have had an unwanted—and very demanding—partner.

But what if Jane turned out to be Ruth's niece? Would Jane allow Ruth into her life, or would she turn her back on both of them, unwilling to let the past intrude on her insulated little world?

If he could convince her to marry him, then nothing that happened would make any difference. It was his only hope.

"I WAS TOLD I COULD find you here."

Peter froze as Mike Morelli slid into the booth across

from him. Denise appeared and handed him a menu. "You want coffee?"

"No, thanks," he said. "A diet soda would be fine, though."

Peter leaned forward, heedless of the bowl of corn chowder in front of him. "What are you doing here? I've been leaving messages with your secretary."

"Looking for you." Mike looked at Peter's soup. "Is that the special today?"

"Yes," Denise announced, plopping the soda in front of the detective. "It comes with a B.L.T. on wheat or white."

Peter looked over to see if Jane was watching. She wasn't. In fact, she had her back to him and a pile of ground sirloin on the counter.

"Sounds good," Mike said, giving her the menu. "White on toast, with extra mayo."

"French fries or potato chips? It comes with chips, but the fries are extra."

"Fries. I might as well live dangerously." He winked at her and watched her walk over to the counter. Then he turned back to Peter. "Is that her?"

"No, thank goodness. And lower your voice. Anyone could hear you."

"I've tried to call you a few times," Mike said, pulling a sheaf of papers from the inside pocket of his jacket. "I have all the information you want."

"Put it away!"

Mike shook his head. "Your family has paid good money for this information. I thought you'd want it right away."

Peter picked up his spoon. "Just act like you're a friend of mine, all right? I don't want to discuss this now."

"The woman?" His eyebrows rose.

"She's the cook here."

"The dark-haired one with the curls?"

"Yes."

Mike nodded. "So *that's* Jane Plainfield."

Peter wanted to ask, but the words stuck in his throat. And this was no place to discuss anything as private as Jane's parentage. No expression crossed Mike's face and the papers lay by his elbow.

Denise brought the bowl of chowder and a packet of oyster crackers and placed them in front of Mike. "There you go. The sandwich will be ready in a sec. Yours, too, Peter."

"Thanks."

Mike grabbed the saltshaker. "Your stepmother has called my office no less than seventeen times."

Peter winced. "I'd hoped to keep her from doing that, but she's pretty independent."

"I did what you said—stalled her until I could talk to you."

"I'm grateful." Peter leaned back as Denise placed the plates of sandwiches in front of them. "Are you a Seahawks fan?"

Mike grinned. "Who isn't?"

"I have season tickets. Let me know when you want to go and I'll send the tickets."

"I appreciate that, but you might want to hear what I found out first."

"Jane?"

Mike nodded. "She's the one."

Peter swore quietly. "You don't know how much I hoped you weren't going to tell me that. And you don't know how complicated this is going to get."

"Look." Mike leaned forward. "What's the problem? Why wouldn't anyone want to know that a rich auntie was looking for her?"

"I don't think she's going to be impressed." Peter looked over toward the grill and saw Jane laughing with one of the elderly fishermen. "And as soon as she finds out I've been lying to her, she's going to kick me out of her life."

"She'll forgive you, once you explain."

"I hope so," Peter muttered. "I want to marry her."

"Don't say I didn't warn you, kid." Mike bit into his sandwich, and for long minutes there was no conversation between the two men. When they were done, Peter tossed a twenty-dollar bill on the table and Mike reached for the papers.

"Come on," he told Mike. "You need to tell me the rest of the story."

Mike waited until they were seated in his Chevrolet sedan before again removing the thick wad of papers from his inner jacket pocket. "Here's a picture of the mother—Lily—in her early twenties. I tracked her to the age of twenty-five. She died in a car accident quite a few years ago."

Peter took the photo with shaking fingers. Once again he knew he had no right to pry into Jane's life. But he did it anyway. It was Ruth's life, too, he reminded himself. A thin woman with yellow, waist-length hair stared back at him. Dressed in torn jeans and a T-shirt with sunflowers painted on it, she looked like any young woman of the late sixties. There was no resemblance to Jane, except for maybe around the mouth. The smile was slightly familiar.

Peter cleared his throat and looked back at the detective. "What else?"

Mike tapped the papers. "The whole story's in there. You already know it. Lily came to Hope in '63, got pregnant and had the baby in Spokane. Gave the baby up for adoption to the Plainfields."

"And the father?"

"Unknown. Though, according to your stepmother, Lily was dating Mitch Parkins all summer."

"Until he died."

"Yeah."

"How'd you find out?"

"Process of elimination, Pete." The detective tapped his finger on his temple. "Used the old brain. I tracked down some employees of the home, and one of them remembered setting up that particular adoption. Seems Lily wanted her child to be raised in Hope, Idaho."

Peter looked down at the photo of the beautiful young woman. "Jane's mother," he murmured. "Wonder what she was thinking with *that* one."

"Well, son, we'll never know, will we?"

"WHERE DID PETER GO?" Jane asked. Denise paused at the cash register and looked out the window.

"He went outside with that friend of his." She stuffed money into her apron pocket. "He sure left a big tip. Didn't even wait for the check."

"That's odd." Jane craned her neck to see into the parking lot. There was no sign of Peter. She hid her disappointment and turned back to the grill. She'd grown accustomed to having him around.

"What are you going to do?"

"I'm not sure." She lowered her voice and moved closer to Denise. "He wants something permanent, but I don't want to get married again—no matter who I fall in love with."

Denise stared at her. "You're really serious?"

Jane picked up the spatula, knowing she needed to get back to the grill, but she continued to wait for Peter to return. "Absolutely serious. Why should I give up everything I have here?"

"Well, that man won't wait around forever, you know." Denise picked up the coffee carafe and moved toward the counter.

"We're not talking about a train."

"No," Denise countered, giving Jane a stern look. "We're talking about a man. A man you're in love with. A man who makes you laugh."

"Shh."

Tim held out his empty coffee cup for Denise to fill. "Are you in love, P.J.?"

"I'm thinking about it," she drawled. "Have you ordered yet?"

"I'll have the special," he said.

"P.J.'s in love?" Roger slid onto the stool next to Tim. He winked at Tim, then turned his attention to Jane. "I heard the Johnson guy is in here all the time. Is this serious? I'm a justice of the peace, you know."

"No, I didn't know. Do you want lunch?"

"The usual."

That was a bacon burger and fries if Mrs. Cantrell wasn't with him, a tuna-fish sandwich with carrot sticks if she was. "Coming right up, as long as you don't ask me any more questions."

"Oh, come on," Tim pleaded. "Everyone's talking about it. Is he here for the summer?" He turned to Roger. "Chet's coming home this week. I wonder what he'll have to say about P.J.'s new boyfriend."

"I'm not discussing this, and if you want something to eat you won't talk about it anymore, either."

"We need ice," Denise said, filling two cups with ginger ale. "Do you want me to get it?"

"No." Jane glared at Tim, who shot her an apologetic look. "I need to get out of here for a minute. Toss a couple of burgers on the grill, will you?" She took the key to the ice machine and slipped out the back door. It was another warm day, but a breeze ruffled her hair and cooled her burning cheeks as she made her way to the side of the building. It was a good day to spend swimming in the lake, she decided, wondering if she really needed to spend the afternoon buying groceries in Sandpoint.

She unlocked the ice machine and opened the door, resisting the urge to stick her head in the opening and inhale the cold air.

"Let me help you with that," Peter said, stepping up beside her.

"All right." She moved out of the way.

"How many?"

"Two." She watched him lift two plastic bags of crushed ice from the cooler. "Thanks." Jane expected him to smile but he didn't. In fact, his eyes looked dark with worry. "Is there something wrong?"

Peter shook his head. "No."

She didn't believe him. "You look upset. Is there anything I can do to help?"

"You can marry me," he stated, standing before her, holding two blue bags of ice. "That would help."

"I've been married before. It's not all it's cracked up to be," she quipped, hoping to make him smile.

"I'm starting to resent being put in the same category as your ex-husband. Can't you see that we're perfect for each other?"

She couldn't argue with that. "Can't we just go on like this?"

"And what happens when the summer is over, Jane? We wave goodbye?"

"We talk on the phone, we visit back and forth. What's wrong with that?"

He set the bags down on the gravel and took Jane by the shoulders. "I can think of a few hundred things that are wrong with that," he growled. "What ever happened to sleeping in the same bed and having children and growing old together?"

She looked up into his serious brown eyes and wished she could believe him. But she'd believed in "till death do us part" once before and look what had happened. She'd been betrayed and humiliated, and since then, she'd learned to depend on no one.

"I'm offering you everything I have," he continued. "I fell in love with you the first time I saw you, from the moment you stepped into that tugboat with me and kissed me all the way across the bay."

"No one falls in love that fast."

"I did."

She groped for something logical to say. "We haven't talked about where we'd live."

"Negotiable, but I'd vote for winters in Boise, summers in Hope."

"And children?"

"Lots."

"And my job?"

"I think your job is a way to keep you from being lonely," Peter said. "And a way to prove to your father that you can take care of things around here."

She winced. "You're not mincing words here, are you?"

"No. I'll have to go back to Boise soon, but I want to make sure that whatever happens doesn't affect the way we feel about each other."

"I fell in love with you," Jane whispered, wondering if he would kiss her. Hoping he would kiss her. "Nothing is going to change that, but—"

"Promise me," he urged. "At least think about it."

"All right."

An expression of relief crossed his face, but his eyes were still dark with worry. "Good."

She gazed up at him until Denise called to her from the back door. "I have to go," she said. "My ice is melting." She picked up the ice, refused his offer of help, and headed toward the back of the restaurant.

"I'll see you later," he called.

Jane didn't turn around. She had to keep her mind on business if she was going to get through the day. How was she going to keep her mind on hamburgers? She wondered if she dared let herself think about marrying him. She'd tried not to, but at odd moments she'd wonder what it would be like to have a child with twinkling brown eyes, to cook breakfast for only one man, to sleep with the sound of someone else breathing beside her.

She wouldn't mind retiring from the restaurant business. But she didn't have to get married to lease the café to someone else. She couldn't imagine living anywhere but Hope, though.

She couldn't imagine life without Peter, either.

He wasn't like Sean, she reminded herself. He wanted her for herself, not for what he thought she owned. Peter Johnson owned a successful business and accepted her for what she was: a small-town girl with a spatula and a trailer. She wasn't beautiful and she wasn't rich, but Peter Johnson loved her.

Jane opened the door with her foot, wishing her workday was finished so she could sit on the dock and think.

"You took long enough," Denise said. "We thought you got run over."

She set the ice on the counter and started prying open the bags. "I was talking to Peter."

"Surprise, surprise. Did he say who his friend was?"

"I didn't ask."

Roger's eyebrows rose. "The short, dark-haired guy that had lunch with him?"

"Yes." Jane looked at him curiously, noting that Denise had cooked his hamburger.

"He's a detective from Spokane. The same guy who was out here a few weeks ago nosing around about Mitch Parkins."

"Who's Mitch Parkins?"

Roger shook his head. "I forget how old you are. Mitch Parkins was your dad's best friend. He died in 1963. Drowned." He paused to wipe his mouth with a paper napkin. "Didn't your dad ever talk about him?"

"I don't remember. The name sounds familiar."

"There used to be a lot of Parkinses," the mayor explained. "The only one who still lived around here died last year."

Denise dumped the ice cubes into the freezer bin. "What would Peter be doing with a detective?"

"He said once that he was trying to find out about his stepmother's family," Jane volunteered. "Maybe it has to do with that." *And the summer of 1963?*

"Think she was a Parkins?" Tim asked.

"I don't know. I'll have to ask him." Jane remembered the worried expression in Peter's eyes. Whatever reason he had for meeting with a detective, he hadn't heard anything that made him happy.

PETER EYED THE PILE of papers in front of him and shoved them all aside, except one. Mitch Parkins, a light-haired giant, stared back at him from the picture Ruth had sent three days ago. He picked up the photo of Lily Simmons and set it carefully beside the one of Mitch.

Jane's parents. The ones she had no interest in finding, she'd told him. And here he was, looking at their pictures and wondering about their lives. Their very short lives.

He would have to tell Ruth, of course. But he'd tell her in person, in Boise.

And she'd fly up here to meet Jane, the long-lost niece.

The picture made him wince. Ruth had as much tact as a prizefighter, and he couldn't see her handling the situation with any kind of finesse.

And if he were Chet Plainfield, he wouldn't want anyone hurting his daughter. Least of all the man who had come up here to find her.

She'd forgive him. Eventually.

And maybe Jane would even enjoy meeting her aunt. They were both outspoken, hardworking, independent women, after all. That's why he loved both of them.

And Jane would be Ruth's only heir, aside from him. That would have to count for something. Although, knowing Jane, he didn't think that would enter into it.

Peter stood and went to the door of the cabin. Through the small window he could see the moonlight rippling on the water. A few stars shone high above the dark outline of the mountains against the sky. It was a beautiful place to live; there was no doubt about that.

But he couldn't stay here forever. In fact, he had no excuses left. He had a business to run, designs to draw, models to test . . . and all the required meetings of a company president.

The summer would soon come to an end, but he didn't want to return to Boise alone.

12

"THE USUAL, DENISE, please." Peter hopped onto the stool next to the one on the end. He glanced at the older man occupying his favorite stool. A tourist, he thought, smiling at Denise as she placed a cup of coffee in front of him.

"There you go," she announced.

"Thanks." Then he raised his voice, watching in appreciation as Jane bent over the grill, her trim little bottom covered in denim. "Good morning, Janie!"

The man beside him turned and gave him a questioning look. Peter ignored him and waited for Jane to turn around.

"Hi!" Her face brightened as she saw him. "I hoped you'd be in early this morning."

"I told you—" He stopped when he saw her shake her head slightly. She didn't want him to finish his sentence, obviously. But he'd had no intention of saying anything even remotely revealing in front of the customers. "I told you," he repeated, his voice lower. "I was going fishing this morning."

A relieved expression crossed her face. "That's right. I forgot. I'll put your eggs on. You want an omelet this morning?"

"Sure."

"Coming up. I have a surprise for you. I'd like you to—"

"Peter? Is that you?"

Peter froze on the stool, not believing the voice he heard behind him. Jane stared past his shoulder toward the door, and the stranger beside him turned on his stool. Peter turned slowly, praying he was hallucinating.

He wasn't. A silver-haired woman in a sleek purple dress and white sandals limped toward him. "Ruth?"

"Well, who else would it be?" She looked around the room as if she was surprised that everyone was staring at her. At eight o'clock in the morning, a woman customer was an unusual sight.

"What are you doing here?" he managed to ask, although he was afraid he knew the answer. Ruth couldn't leave well enough alone, and he dreaded what would happen next.

"Well, dear, we have some things to talk about." She slid onto the stool at his left, and he swiveled around to face her.

"Don't sit down! This isn't the time or the place—"

"After breakfast, then," she agreed, settling herself on the stool. "Are you eating?" He nodded, and she waved to Denise. "A cup of tea, please. And make sure the water is boiling before you pour it over the tea bag, thank you."

"No problem," Denise said, pulling a cup from the shelf. "I can make tea."

Peter kept his voice low, hoping Ruth would realize she shouldn't discuss anything private within hearing distance of every fisherman in Hope, Idaho. "How did you get here?"

"I flew into Spokane last night and hired a car. You know I'm an early riser. Pass me the sugar, dear."

He did as he was told and watched his stepmother fix her tea. Her long hair waved neatly to her chin, and her big blue eyes were neatly made up. She always looked as if she'd just stepped out of a beauty salon. "But your hip," he stammered. "I thought you were supposed to stay off it."

She sniffed. "It's been weeks, Peter. I think you've lost track of time." She took a sip of her tea and nodded appreciatively. "Good. Nice and hot."

"But Ruth—"

"Your breakfast," Jane stated, placing his plate in front of him. "Just the way you like it." She gave him a cheerful grin and shot Ruth a curious look before turning back to Peter. "When you have a minute, there's someone I want you to meet."

Peter nodded and moved his plate closer. "Thanks. This looks great."

"Honey," the man next to him said. "Pour a little more coffee in this cup, would you? I think I'll stick around a little longer."

"Now," Ruth began, swiveling to face her stepson. "Tell me everything you know about Jane Plainfield."

Jane stopped pouring coffee and stared at them.

Peter's fork clattered to the plate. "Ruth, I don't—"

"There's no denying it," she declared, interrupting him once again. "I bullied that detective into telling me the name. Reminded him who was paying the bills in this investigation."

"Investigation?" Jane repeated. "What is she talking about, Peter?"

"Young lady," Ruth began, clearly aggravated by the interruption. "If you don't mind, this is a private conversation."

Jane glared back at her. "Not when you're talking about me, it isn't."

"You?" Ruth's eyes brightened, then a confused expression crossed her face. "It can't be. You don't look anything like him."

Jane frowned. "Like who?" She turned to Peter. "What is this woman talking about? And who *is* she, anyway?"

The man next to Peter swiveled to face them. "I know who she is," he declared, his suntanned face creasing into a myriad frown lines. He glared past Peter to the woman drinking her tea. "Ruth Parkins. You always had quite a mouth for a little girl."

Ruth's teacup clattered to the saucer. "Chet Plainfield," she declared, unperturbed by his frown. "I would never have recognized you. Except the voice is the same, of course," she sniffed. "I'd recognize that *tone* anywhere."

"Never mind my tone. What do you want with my daughter?"

Chet Plainfield? Peter stared at the man beside him, wishing he could have met him ten minutes earlier. Now everything was going to blow up, and he didn't know how he could stop it from happening. He'd hoped he could have avoided this, and only Chet could have helped him do it.

"Your daughter?" Ruth nodded. "I wondered, when I heard the name. But it seemed like too much of a coincidence."

Jane put her hands on her hips and glared at the three of them. "Would someone tell me what is going on around here?"

Ruth ignored her question. "You know why I'm here. For Mitch."

Denise approached the counter, an order slip in her hand. "Three orders of hotcakes and a scrambled with ham. Want me to start making it?"

Jane nodded. "Yes."

"Let's get out of here," Peter suggested, leaving his uneaten breakfast.

"Who the hell are you?" Chet asked him. "And why should I go anywhere with you?"

"He's a friend," Jane said, frowning. "At least, I thought he was."

"My stepson," Ruth answered.

"I'm going to marry your daughter," Peter announced.

Jane tossed her apron on the counter. "Is that why you had me investigated?"

"No, but—"

Ruth stood, calmly wiping her lips with a paper napkin. "That was my idea, dear. I wanted to find you, you see. You're my only living relative, so you're very important to me."

Chet took Ruth's arm. "*Out.*"

"What?"

"Get out. Now."

"You can't do that," she huffed. "Peter!"

Peter took her elbow. "Come on. You've caused enough trouble by coming here. Let's go over to my cabin and talk this over."

"I'm coming, too," Jane insisted.

"Don't worry," Denise said. "I can manage everything here."

Chet stopped Jane as she stepped around the counter. "I don't want you talking to that old woman."

"Why not?"

A shadow crossed his face. "What's in the past should be left in the past."

Jane took his hand. "Daddy—"

"Your father's right," Peter said, touching her shoulder to get her attention. "Let it be."

She shook her head and looked past him toward Ruth. "No. She's started something. Let's finish it."

"I don't want anything to do with this," her father declared, his voice heavy with unspoken emotion. He stood and frowned at his daughter. "I'm your father, and I always have been."

"What are you talking about?" Jane's eyes filled with tears. "Of course, you're my father. Nothing could ever change that."

"You don't know—"

Peter, conscious of the curious stares around them, guided Chet to the door. "Let's talk outside."

"No," Jane said. "We'll go to Dad's. It's closer."

Chet sighed, shoved his large hands into his pants pockets and led the way. Jane hurried after him, while Peter took Ruth's arm and guided her across the rough driveway.

"I thought you were going to let me handle this," he said in a low voice.

"You weren't telling me the truth."

"I would have. Eventually."

Ruth's hand tightened on his arm. "Don't look so grim, darling. Everyone knows that it's better to tell the truth."

"The truth," Jane said, looking at Peter for help. "You have to tell me what's going on." She didn't know who this older woman was, except that she was Peter's stepmother and for some reason Dad knew her. And that she was a woman used to giving orders and having things her own way. Jane eyed Ruth as she took a seat on the sofa. Peter ignored the space beside her, and instead sat on a hassock he pulled close to Jane's chair.

"That's not so easy," Chet declared, still frowning. He leaned against the hearth and glared at Ruth. "And not necessary, either. If people would mind their own business, that is."

"*I* think it's necessary. And long overdue," Ruth sniffed. She turned to Jane, and her expression softened. "I would never do anything to hurt you, my dear. You do know you're adopted, don't you?"

Jane felt her stomach muscles tense. "I've always known. It never really mattered. That's what this is all about, isn't it?" Was this woman her birth mother? She didn't think so. She thought there would have been some kind of instant connection, but maybe that just happened in books.

Ruth nodded. "I think I'm your aunt." She glanced at Peter, who reached for Jane's hand. "I hired a detective to find you. He and my stepson have been working for weeks trying to locate you."

"But I've always been here, always been me," Jane protested, wondering why she felt so numb. She let Peter hold her hands between his and wondered why her fingers were cold. She looked over at her father. "Dad, what's going on?"

He didn't look at her, but eyed Ruth. "Go ahead, Ruth. Let's hear what you have to say."

"All right," she said, clearing her throat. "In 1963 a young woman came to Hope to visit her godmother, who had had surgery and needed her help. The girl's name was Lily Simmons, and she and my brother Mitch fell in love. Mitch drowned out on the lake later that summer—a freak storm came up while he was fishing. And Lily found out she was pregnant."

Jane leaned forward, trying to absorb what she'd been told. "And you think I'm that baby?"

Ruth nodded. "I'm sure of it. Lily had no choice but to go to an unwed mothers' home in Spokane and put the baby up for adoption." She looked over at Chet. "Isn't that right, Chet?"

"Yes," he whispered. "She had no choice."

"Dad?" Her father had turned pale under his tan, and his fingers were clenched tightly by his sides. "Are you all right?"

He tried to smile, but failed miserably. "I'm okay." He looked back at Ruth. "Are you finished?"

Her eyebrows rose. "I'm sorry you feel so threatened, Chet. I didn't intend to hurt anyone by this, but—"

"Why now?" Chet asked. "Why—after thirty years—do you have to poke your nose into something that doesn't concern you?"

Jane waited for the older woman's answer. She didn't think Ruth was the kind of woman to keep a secret for thirty years. "Yes, Ruth," she urged. "What could you possibly want from me after all these years?"

"You're the only one left," she answered, her eyes filling with tears. "I adored my older brother, and after he died nothing was ever the same. I didn't know about you, you see, until my sister died last year. There were letters in her desk, and her diary.... Imagine my surprise when I learned that there were rumors about Mitch and a pregnant girlfriend! I *had* to find you. I thought you might want to know about your father." She shot an apologetic look at Chet, who hadn't moved from his place in front of the hearth. "Your *birth* father, I mean."

Was there something she was supposed to feel? Jane looked down at her hands clasped in Peter's and she tugged them away. He'd come to Hope to solve a mystery, but he had lied to her all along. Her voice was quiet as she looked down at him. "What does this have to do with us?"

"Nothing," he declared, his dark eyes serious for a change. "I promised my stepmother I would help discover what happened to Lily Simmons's baby. And I did."

"You've been lying to me all along." Strange, how that hurt the most. Her heart began to ache.

"I didn't want you to get hurt. All along I hoped you weren't the right one, that you had nothing to do with Ruth's search. But—"

"You lied," she repeated, looking away from him. She couldn't bear to see the sincere expression in his eyes and know that it was so easily assumed. "You've been lying and I've believed everything you've said."

"My dear," Ruth interjected. "Peter had no other choice. He had to be sure before he told you about this. You're my only relative now, and I have a very substantial estate."

"I don't want your money," Jane whispered. She stood and moved away from Peter. "I think you'd better go," she told him. "You've done what you came here to do."

Ruth stood, too. "You need some time to absorb all of this, of course. I'll be staying with the Stones at the Rainbow Resort for a few days. I'd like to tell you about your father. I brought pictures. There aren't very many, but—"

"*Stop*," Chet commanded. He pointed to the picture above the fireplace and his voice shook. "*That* man is Jane's father."

"Of course you are, Daddy," Jane assured him. "They're going to leave now, and—"

"No." He shook his head. "You don't understand. You're no relation to Ruth or Mitch Parkins."

"But—" Ruth stammered, and sank back into the couch.

Peter nodded. "Why don't you tell the whole story, Mr. Plainfield?"

Chet took Jane by the hand and led her back to the chair. He sat on its arm, not releasing his grip on Jane's fingers. "It was 1963, all right. And Lily Simmons came to Hope, just as you said." His voice lowered. "She was beautiful. Tall and blond, smart . . . an artist. With a sweet smile and a kind way about her." He smiled down at Jane. "Your mother," he declared. "That much is true." He cleared his throat before he could continue.

"You loved her, too?" Ruth gasped.

"Yes. And she loved me."

Jane held her breath and stared at her father. "But you were married," she said after a long moment.

"Yes. I was married. And I fell in love with Lily Simmons that summer of '63, and she had my child." He took a deep breath. "I was filled with guilt. I'd betrayed my wife, and my best friend, too. Mitch was in love with her, too. They'd dated a few times, but no one knew we loved each other, although I think there were some that may have suspected." He squeezed Jane's hand. "There was nothing I could do to help Lily, except adopt my own daughter. Lily thought that was the perfect solution, and Ethel . . . Well, Ethel forgave me. We hadn't been able to have children and you were a dream come true."

"Mom called me her 'little miracle,'" Jane whispered.

"And you were," her father agreed. "To both of us."

"What happened to Lily?"

Peter spoke up for the first time. "She died in a car accident when she was twenty-five years old. She had become an artist, which was what she wanted. I've researched her work. Some of her pieces, especially the watercolors, have become quite valuable."

"She would have liked that," Chet said. "I knew she'd died, which is why I never told you about her," he explained. "There didn't seem to be any reason anymore."

"What about Mom? Did you love her?" It was very important to hear his answer. She'd thought her parents shared a wonderful kind of love. Could that have been a lie, too?

"Yes, very much. We worked hard to repair our marriage. She was a very special woman."

Ruth finally spoke. Her voice quavered as she asked, "Then Jane isn't my niece, after all?"

"No," Chet said. "I felt Mitch deserved to know the truth, so I told him. He punched me in the nose, knocked me down, in fact. I never saw him again. I'm sorry, Ruth."

She shook her head, and opened her purse. After she'd wiped her eyes, she turned to Jane. "I owe you an apology, my dear. I invaded your privacy, which was unforgivable, in the light of everything."

Jane went over to her and knelt down in front of her. "I'm glad you wanted to know me that much," she assured her. "At least I know that it would have been important to my birth mother, too. After all, if an aunt wanted to find me that much, think what my birth mother would have done." She smiled, and Ruth answered with one of her own.

"You're a Plainfield, plain as day," the woman declared. "Though, damn it, I wish you weren't."

"Thanks." Jane took the hand the older woman offered. "I think."

"Come, Peter," Ruth said, rising from the couch. "I think we should leave now."

"Not yet," Peter said. "I need to talk to Jane."

"No," Jane said, fighting to ignore the pain around her heart. "I don't think we have anything to say. In fact, I want you to leave. Now."

"No," he said, stepping closer. "You have to hear me out."

Jane wanted to punch him in the mouth. An appropriate place, since that mouth had told her lies and smiled and kissed her and made love to her...and asked her to marry him.

Lies, all of it. Her hands balled into fists at her sides as she stood and glared at him. "If you won't go, I will."

Chet put his arm around her, forming a united front as they faced Ruth's stepson. "I think you'd better do what my daughter says."

Peter's mouth hardened into a thin line, but he stepped back and guided Ruth through the living room and out the door. Jane waited until she heard the kitchen door close before she spoke.

"I'm sorry, Dad. For everything."

"That's supposed to be my line," he said, pulling her into his arms. She wrapped her arms around her father's waist and tried to hold back the tears. Overwhelming grief for the mother she'd never known threatened to drown her, while the stark pain of Peter's betrayal left her shaking with despair.

"There's a lot to tell you," her father said.

"Yes," she agreed. "We have a lot to talk about." She wanted to know everything about Lily Simmons and the summer her father fell in love.

"I DIDN'T THINK I'd find you here." Peter stood on the dock and watched Jane coil rope into neat loops—an evening chore usually done by Tim. "Your father wouldn't tell me where you'd gone."

She didn't look up at him. "I needed the air."

"You also need an explanation."

"I've heard enough for one day." Jane turned away, heading toward the boats lined up along the narrow walkway. Peter followed her and caught her by the elbow.

"Come on," he ordered, leading her to his boat.

"No." She tried to dig in her heels, but he was too strong for her. He gave her no choice. She could step into the boat or else fall into the lake. "What the hell do you think you're trying to prove?" she demanded, her eyes flashing as he got in beside her.

He didn't answer. He knew their voices would carry over the water, and he had no intention of entertaining the tourists or the fishermen with his explanation—and everything else he had to say. He untied the boat from the moorings and pushed off from the dock before starting the engine. Jane scrambled to her seat and gripped the dashboard.

Peter didn't speak until he'd guided the boat into the bay. Once he'd reached the open water, he cut the engine with the prow facing the sun hovering above the western mountains. Somehow he had to make her understand, even if he had to sit in the middle of the bay for the entire evening.

"I didn't lie," he announced. "I told you I was doing research."

She turned to him, and he realized her eyes were slightly puffy, as if she'd been crying for a long, long time. He wanted to wrap her in his arms and hold her forever, but he stopped himself from trying. She'd probably just belt him. "You didn't tell me you were doing research about *me*. What did you hope to gain from all this, Peter?"

"I promised Ruth I'd contact the detective she'd hired. I never dreamed I'd meet someone like you."

"Pretty convenient, wasn't it?" Her eyes looked bleak. "What were you trying to do? Marry the heiress? Keep the business in the family? You used me, Peter. You made love to me and never told me why you were here, or who I was." Her voice broke, and she turned away from him and wiped her eyes.

"I wanted to marry Jane Plainfield," he said, hoping for the words that would make her believe him. "I didn't know you were the one when I asked you to marry me. In fact, I hoped like hell you weren't."

She turned back to him. "Why?"

"Because, my love, I knew this would come between us. I'd hoped to avoid it. Hoped someone else would be Ruth's missing relative."

"A relative who didn't exist." She sighed. "Is she very disappointed?"

"Yes, but I promised her grandchildren. Soon. I left her having drinks with Don and Linda on their deck. Do you want to get married here in Hope?"

"I'm not marrying you," she replied, but her voice shook when she said the words. "You lied. You never told me who I was, never told me the truth."

"It wasn't my story to tell." He leaned forward and took her by the shoulders. "I knew you were Chet Plainfield's daughter when I saw his picture over the fireplace the day after we camped at the Monarchs. Of course I didn't know the whole story, but I knew you weren't related to Ruth. I wanted to talk to your father before I told her." He watched the disbelieving expression cross her face and he wanted to shake her.

"But how did you know?"

"The pictures," he explained. "I'd seen one of Lily, and you didn't look like her, except for the smile. And I'd had Ruth send me a photo of Mitch Parkins. Again, no resemblance. But there was the picture of your father, with his curly dark hair and his light eyes and the stubborn chin." He touched her chin. "Very familiar." Then he smiled, hoping she'd smile back; but she remained serious and doubting. "There was more to the story, you see, and it wasn't my story to tell."

"You want me to believe you were waiting for my father?"

"I want you to believe I love you," he tried.

She shook her head. "No. You wanted information. You wanted to marry the woman who might inherit Ruth's share of your business."

"What?" Peter started to laugh.

Jane glared at him. "What's so funny?"

"Ruth doesn't own the business. I do. She's one of the vice presidents and managers, but Baysider is mine. Ruth owns three restaurants in Boise, apartment buildings in Pocatello and a ski resort north of Seattle, but she doesn't own Baysider."

"Then what did you want from me?"

"Only to love you forever," he whispered.

"There's no such thing as 'forever,'" she said, refusing to meet his gaze.

Peter's patience snapped. "Fine," he conceded, feeling his anger rise. "You're so damned independent, then live that way." He turned the key in the ignition and started the boat's engine. "If you'd rather have customers than children, a trailer instead of a permanent home, and a restaurant instead of a family, then that's your choice. You've wrapped yourself up in your nice safe little world and told yourself that you're happy. Well, I don't think you're so happy." He increased the pressure on the throttle and turned the boat toward shore. "I think you're so afraid of getting hurt that you won't come out of that cozy shell you've wrapped yourself in. Well, you're welcome to it."

Jane remained silent, the breeze blowing her curls around her face as the sun set in rosy streaks behind her. It was a heart-wrenching final image of what had been the best four weeks of his life.

HE LEFT HER AT THE DOCK, and Jane watched him stride up the walkway toward the café. He would head back to the Rainbow Resort, she knew, and would probably pack up his things and leave.

Tim stepped out of the supply shed. "Lose a customer, P.J.?"

"I guess I have." Her heart felt heavy enough to sink to her toes.

"Too bad. I was starting to like him."

"Me, too," she replied, watching Peter round a corner and disappear from her sight. Was he right? Had she used her damned independence as an excuse to keep from falling in love? Well, she'd fallen in love despite her struggles not to. And look where it had landed her. Sitting on the dock of the bay, like the Otis Redding song said.

Alone. Which was what she wanted. Jane frowned as she looked across the lake at the Monarchs rising out of the water. Hadn't she gotten exactly what she wanted?

"Tim," she called, scrambling to her feet. She'd have to hurry before the light disappeared. "Do you have any cans of marine paint around here?"

"YOU'RE AS NERVOUS AS a cat at a dog show," Denise observed. "What's the matter with you?"

Jane looked out the window for the fiftieth time. Or maybe the hundredth. "I'm waiting for Peter to come in."

"Are you going to marry him one of these days or what?"

"Yes, if he ever comes in here so I can tell him."

Denise grinned. "How do you know he hasn't left town? I heard you two broke up and he was heading back to Boise with that stepmother of his."

"News sure travels fast." She poured herself another cup of coffee. "Don said he'd give Peter the message."

"Well, you've got three orders up, so maybe you'd better start cracking some eggs." Denise pinned the slips of paper to the hood of the grill. "These customers won't wait forever."

Jane froze as Peter pushed open the door and walked toward her. His expression was carefully guarded, though he didn't seem to notice the curious looks the fishermen gave him. He carried a large flat package under his arm, which he leaned against the end stool when he stepped up to the counter.

"I got your message," he said, and waited for her to explain.

"I have something for you," she managed to say, hoping he would at least smile. He didn't. "The boat," she began, but he interrupted her.

"You can rip up the lease," he said. "I won't be back."

"Are you sure?"

He nodded, and slid the package around the counter. "Watch out. You don't want to get anything spilled on it."

"What is it?"

"Something I tracked down last week, before—well, before everything happened." He put his hands in his pockets and waited as she tore off the brown paper covering.

Jane gasped. In her hands was a watercolor painting, framed in a simple gold frame. A riot of color—a mountain meadow filled with waving yellow bear grass, a soft blue lake, and distant mountains—filled the canvas. And in the corner was a simple signature: L. Simmons. "My mother?"

Peter cleared his throat. "Yes." He turned to leave.

Denise put a cup of coffee on the counter for him. "You're not going to have breakfast?"

He shook his head. "No. Not today."

Jane tore her gaze from the painting and looked up at Peter. "Thank you."

"You're welcome." He almost smiled. "I'm glad you like it."

"I have something for you," she said, pulling off her apron. "Here, Denise, it's all yours. You've always wanted to lease this place. Here's your chance, starting today."

Denise took the apron and wrapped it around her waist. "You have yourself a deal."

Jane took Peter's hand and led him outside. For once, he didn't have anything to say, she noted. Her heart felt lighter and lighter by the second as she led him down to the dock.

"There," she said, pointing to the Baysider. "I named the boat."

Stenciled on the stern were the neat letters, *Lucky Lady*.

"You're going to keep her, then?"

Jane shook her head. "No. I finally figured out what to do with her. I'm giving her to you."

He frowned down at her. "I don't get it."

She reached up and traced his lips with her finger. "It's a wedding present." She watched as understanding crossed his face. Finally his dark eyes began to twinkle.

"Are you proposing to me, Jane Plainfield?"

"I guess I am, yes."

He wrapped his arms around her. "How do you know I'll say yes?"

She reached up and put her arms around his neck. "Oh, I know I can't lose," she murmured, as his lips descended close to hers. "This is my lucky day."

"Oh, yeah?" He stopped a bare inch above her mouth. "I think *I'm* the lucky one. After all, I just got a boat *and* the woman. How much luckier can a man get?"

Jane smiled and tugged him closer. "Kiss me and find out."

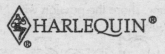

THE VENGEFUL GROOM
Sara Wood

Legend has it that those married in Eternity's chapel are destined for a lifetime of happiness. But happiness isn't what Giovanni wants from marriage—it's revenge!

Ten years ago, Tina's testimony sent Gio to prison—for a crime he didn't commit. *Now* he's back in Eternity and looking for a bride. *Now* Tina is about to learn just how ruthless and disturbingly sensual Gio's brand of vengeance can be.

THE VENGEFUL GROOM, available in October from Harlequin Presents, is the fifth book in Harlequin's new cross-line series, **WEDDINGS, INC.** Be sure to look for the sixth book, **EDGE OF ETERNITY,** by Jasmine Cresswell (Harlequin Intrigue #298), coming in November.

WED5

This November, share the passion with *New York Times* Bestselling Author

(previously published under the pseudonym Erin St. Claire)

in

THE DEVIL'S OWN

Kerry Bishop was a good samaritan with a wild plan. Linc O'Neal was a photojournalist with a big heart.

Their scheme to save nine orphans from a hazardos land was foolhardy at best—deadly at the worst.

But together they would battle the odds—and the burning hungers—that made the steamy days and sultry nights doubly dangerous.

Reach for the brightest star in women's fiction with

MIRA

HARLEQUIN®

Temptation®

HART GIRLS

Bestselling Temptation author Elise Title is back
with a funny, sexy trilogy—THE HART GIRLS—
written in the vein of her popular miniseries
THE FORTUNE BOYS!

Rachel, Julie and Kate Hart are three women of the
nineties with heart and spark. They're determined
to win the TV ratings wars—and win the men of
their dreams!

Stay tuned for:

#509 DANGEROUS AT HEART (October 1994)
#513 HEARTSTRUCK (November 1994)
#517 HEART TO HEART (December 1994)

Available wherever Harlequin books are sold.

This September, discover the fun of falling in love with...

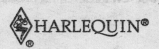
love and laughter

Harlequin is pleased to bring you this exciting new collection of three original short stories by bestselling authors!

ELISE TITLE
BARBARA BRETTON
LASS SMALL

LOVE AND LAUGHTER—sexy, romantic, fun stories guaranteed to tickle your funny bone and fuel your fantasies!

Available in September wherever
Harlequin books are sold.

◆ HARLEQUIN ®

1994 MISTLETOE MARRIAGES
HISTORICAL CHRISTMAS STORIES

With a twinkle of lights and a flurry of snowflakes,
Harlequin Historicals presents *Mistletoe Marriages,* a
collection of four of the most magical stories by your favorite
historical authors. The perfect way to celebrate the season!

Brimming with romance and good cheer, these heartwarming
stories will be available in November wherever Harlequin
books are sold.

RENDEZVOUS by Elaine Barbieri
THE WOLF AND THE LAMB by Kathleen Eagle
CHRISTMAS IN THE VALLEY by Margaret Moore
KEEPING CHRISTMAS by Patricia Gardner Evans

Add a touch of romance to your holiday with
Mistletoe Marriages Christmas Stories!

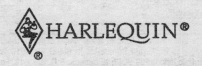

HARLEQUIN®

MMXS94

RIGHT MAN...WRONG TIME

Remember that one man who turned your world upside down? Who made you experience all the ecstatic highs of passion and lows of loss and regret. What if you met him again?

If you missed any Lost Loves titles, here's your chance to order them:

Harlequin Temptation®—Lost Loves

#25589	THE RETURN OF CAINE O'HALLORAN by JoAnn Ross	$2.99	☐
#25593	WHAT MIGHT HAVE BEEN by Glenda Sanders	$2.99 U.S. $3.50 CAN.	☐ ☐
#25600	FORMS OF LOVE by Rita Clay Estrada	$2.99 U.S. $3.50 CAN.	☐ ☐
#25601	GOLD AND GLITTER by Gina Wilkins	$2.99 U.S. $3.50 CAN.	☐ ☐
#25605	EVEN COWBOYS GET THE BLUES by Carin Rafferty	$2.99 U.S. $3.50 CAN.	☐ ☐

(limited quantities available on certain titles)

TOTAL AMOUNT	$
POSTAGE & HANDLING	$
($1.00 for one book, 50¢ for each additional)	
APPLICABLE TAXES*	$_____
TOTAL PAYABLE	$_____
(check or money order—please do not send cash)	

To order, complete this form and send it, along with a check or money order for the total above, payable to Harlequin Books, to: **In the U.S.:** 3010 Walden Avenue, P.O. Box 9047, Buffalo, NY 14269-9047; **In Canada:** P.O. Box 613, Fort Erie, Ontario, L2A 5X3.

Name: _____

Address: _____ City: _____

State/Prov.: _____ Zip/Postal Code: _____

*New York residents remit applicable sales taxes.
Canadian residents remit applicable GST and provincial taxes.

LOSTF

MIRA™

The brightest star in women's fiction!

This October, reach for the stars and watch all your dreams come true with **MIRA BOOKS.**

HEATHER GRAHAM POZZESSERE
Slow Burn in October
An enthralling tale of murder and passion set against the dark and glittering world of Miami.

SANDRA BROWN
The Devil's Own in November
She made a deal with the devil…but she didn't bargain on losing her heart.

BARBARA BRETTON
Tomorrow & Always in November
Unlikely lovers from very different worlds… They had to cross time to find one another.

PENNY JORDAN
For Better For Worse in December
Three couples, three dreams—can they rekindle the love and passion that first brought them together?

The sky has no limit with **MIRA BOOKS.**

HARLEQUIN®

Don't miss these Harlequin favorites by some of our most distinguished authors!
And now you can receive a discount by ordering two or more titles!

HT #25525	THE PERFECT HUSBAND by Kristine Rolofson	$2.99 ☐
HT #25554	LOVERS' SECRETS by Glenda Sanders	$2.99 ☐
HP #11577	THE STONE PRINCESS by Robyn Donald	$2.99 ☐
HP #11554	SECRET ADMIRER by Susan Napier	$2.99 ☐
HR #03277	THE LADY AND THE TOMCAT by Bethany Campbell	$2.99 ☐
HR #03283	FOREIGN AFFAIR by Eva Rutland	$2.99 ☐
HS #70529	KEEPING CHRISTMAS by Marisa Carroll	$3.39 ☐
HS #70578	THE LAST BUCCANEER by Lynn Erickson	$3.50 ☐
HI #22256	THRICE FAMILIAR by Caroline Burnes	$2.99 ☐
HI #22238	PRESUMED GUILTY by Tess Gerritsen	$2.99 ☐
HAR #16496	OH, YOU BEAUTIFUL DOLL by Judith Arnold	$3.50 ☐
HAR #16510	WED AGAIN by Elda Minger	$3.50 ☐
HH #28719	RACHEL by Lynda Trent	$3.99 ☐
HH #28795	PIECES OF SKY by Marianne Willman	$3.99 ☐

Harlequin Promotional Titles

#97122	LINGERING SHADOWS by Penny Jordan	$5.99 ☐
	(limited quantities available on certain titles)	

	AMOUNT	$
DEDUCT:	10% DISCOUNT FOR 2+ BOOKS	$
	POSTAGE & HANDLING	$
	($1.00 for one book, 50¢ for each additional)	
	APPLICABLE TAXES*	$_____
	TOTAL PAYABLE	$_____
	(check or money order—please do not send cash)	

To order, complete this form and send it, along with a check or money order for the total above, payable to Harlequin Books, to: **In the U.S.:** 3010 Walden Avenue, P.O. Box 9047, Buffalo, NY 14269-9047; **In Canada:** P.O. Box 613, Fort Erie, Ontario, L2A 5X3.

Name: _____

Address:_____ City: _____

State/Prov.: _____ Zip/Postal Code: _____

*New York residents remit applicable sales taxes.
Canadian residents remit applicable GST and provincial taxes..

HBACK-JS